The Bizarchives
Weird Tales of Monsters, Magic, and Machines

Cosmic Horror Double Feature

DREADGE
&
PRESTWICK'S PROJECT

by A. Cuthbertson

PRESENTED BY
THE MIDGARD INSTITUTE
OF SCIENCE FICTION & FANTASY LITERATURE

Table of Contents

Preface

In the golden era of fiction during the early 20th century there was a toiling primordial soup of forming genres and subgenres that seemed to blend and blur without rhyme or reason. It was an age of literary experimentation and innovation. Science fiction, sword and sorcery, mobster noirs, and thrilling creature features could be found in abundance among the uncountable pulp publications of yesteryear.

One of the most beloved genres not just of pulp but throughout history was the tradition of spooky storytelling. It started as campfire folklore tales about witches and monsters, then gradually evolved into multi-million dollar horror cinema. To this day we are obsessed with tall tales about cryptids, paranormal phenomena, and terror of supernatural quality.

However, one writer conceptualized a form of terror that changed our understanding forevermore. This man was HP Lovecraft, and his genre is now aptly dubbed "Cosmic Horror". It was a revolutionary approach to horror writing that made former tales of hauntings and swamp creatures seem helplessly insignificant.

Also sometimes called "Lovecraftian horror", this tradition skips the gore and ghouls and calls into question man's existence on an ontological level. It twists our understanding of reality itself with mockeries of nature and unfathomable scales. It assaults man's ego and grinds his self-image into an inconsequential grain of sand among an endless ocean of cosmic proportions.

After Lovecraft's unfortunately early passing, his innovative style became wildly popular. For many decades films, comics, movies, and every other possible media medium adopted the aesthetic. And unfortunately few manage to capture the magic of cosmic horror as it once was. With either counterfeit retellings of his stories or commercialized and commodified garbage with cutsie octopus headed-characters, few hold the proverbial silver key to Lovecraft's inspiration.

Here we bring you two tales that have rightfully earned their place as organic and earnest works of traditional cosmic horror. They're neither copycat knockoffs nor an expansion of previous mythos. "Dreadge" and "Prestwick's Project" build off of Lovecraftian cosmicism but are fresh and original in their own right. A. Cuthbertson does a masterful job of reinvigorating the genre in his own way with his British flavor.

Here he shines a light on the historical struggles of the English working class and critiques the follies of modern celebrity science. But he does so without the forced propaganda-signaling found in most literature today. He does so tastefully and demonstrably through good ol' fashioned storytelling.

With these works, A. Cuthbertson solidifies himself as a proper heir of the Lovecraftian tradition and one of the most exciting upcoming fiction authors of our era.

Prepare yourself for a journey into the unspeakably weird from one of the strangest sons of The Bizarchives.

D.R.E.A.D.G.E

I: To Wickern Fen

I'm telling you, at first I thought those Fen Tigers were just a bunch of old sticks-in-the-mud. But I've never seen anyone fight harder for their land. They were fierce and mean. They really earned the name Tigers, although their ferocity did them no good in the end, did it?

We made sure of that, as much as I wish we hadn't. I wish I'd never taken on that job, but the pay was too good, and, besides, I didn't know what I was getting into at the time.

What's a Fen Tiger, you're asking? Well, you'd be forgiven for not knowing. I didn't know either.

They were men, not tigers, using the name to scare people away. Although they dispersed pretty quickly themselves after the events at Wickern Fen. They melted into the mud, faded into the fog.

The more you tried to grab hold of them, the quicker they slipped out of your grasp. And after that one horrid night, they were never seen again.

Go down to Cambridge, and go the taverns, go to the inns, walk around the market in the middle of the day and ask anybody: have you heard of the Fen Tigers? You'll be met with stony silence. In fact, they'll walk away; they'll pretend you're not even there.

How word travels so fast among those folk, I'll never know. You ask something of one of those backwater bumpkins, and the whole bloody town knows you're asking. Very inconvenient in my line of work.

We were sent into the Fenland from London. We were all looking for jobs, having just been shipped back from some transport strike in Liverpool. A crowd had gathered there, no less than eighty thousand, to hear some syndicalist rabble-rouser do a speech. It got rowdy, to say the least.

The police couldn't handle it, so we were employed to be the "tough guys" up at the front. "Crowd dispersal," you know? They'd outfit us in police uniforms and give us truncheons and let us loose. Great fun.

And if anybody complained? Well, the next day, there was nobody at fault, was there? Those heavy-handed officers didn't exist anymore. They were on the train home, laughing, with heavy pockets. The history books emit references to folk like us, and we're happy about it.

Anyway, we were a gang of enforcers, mercenaries for the government, or simply for the highest bidder. Often, they were one and the same. Some of our group didn't care for that label, "mercenary," preferring such grand titles as "additional enforcement officers."

Me? I was just a big, unscrupulous bastard, and I'd do anything for the pay. I didn't give a damn what they called me. The things I'd see in the Fen would turn me away from that line of work, but back then, I didn't give a hoot.

I got off the train in London, spent my pay in pubs and brothels, and before the week was out, I was back at my agent's place chasing down my next job. There was plenty of the usual stuff. A few quid here and there for shaking down a union boss. A few shillings to stand near some protesters and look menacing.

But one opportunity in particular caught my attention straight away. I could live off that pay packet for months. It was an invitation from somebody calling himself a "gentleman adventurer." Dutch fella by the name of Van Buskirk.

Apparently he was an entrepreneurial young man who wanted to "secure some farmland". My agent told me he'd made a pretty penny reclaiming farmland from the sea for the Dutch government… using some kind of advanced engineering. Lord knows how he managed that, I remember thinking. Must have been a real brainbox.

The job wasn't too far away from London, anyway. A small village called Wickern, apparently quite remote, one of a few such hamlets in the Fens over Cambridge way.

I'd never been, but for the money Van Buskirk was offering, I'd have gone a lot further. I passed the word on to the lads, and by the next morning, ten of us were on the train over to Cambridge.

It was a secretive operation, to be sure. We knew nothing of the details of the job when we took it on, but we knew how to read between the lines by now: "securing land" meant removing its rightful owners by coercion. Our patron, our gentlemen adventurer, would be a puppet funded by somebody in Parliament. There might be some police support, but nothing like up in Liverpool.

Thing is, nobody was trying to hide the unrest in Liverpool. Quite the opposite. The more attention from the press, the better.

We'd been told that the situation in the Fens was rather different… the locals wanted the authorities out; sure, they wanted the venture capitalists out, of course, and they even chased the land surveyors out. Hell, you couldn't even plant a spy -- they sniffed them a mile off.

If somebody walks into a tavern out there, in the Fens, and they aren't from the area, well… every eyeball in the place swivels towards the doorway. The chatter ceases. The darts stop in mid-air. You know places like that, I'm sure.

Anyway, this was nothing new in the kind of communities we were sent to disrupt. But this was the strange thing about Wickern: they didn't want any journalists involved, either. Reporters were sent packing, often with a bloody nose and considerably lighter pockets. Normally, these places wanted all the help they could get, all the outrage that a newspaper could ignite among the rest of the populace.

But no -- the people of Wickern had something to hide. A secret to keep. Maybe this Van Buskirk knew what it was, maybe he didn't. The lads didn't care, but I was intrigued - what could a backwater bog-village possibly have to keep secret? What was under those murky waters?

Certainly not riches, or else none of them would live there, would they? They'd be here in London spending it all. No, there was something else, and I was determined to winkle it out.

I pulled my hat over my eyes and leaned back in my seat until our train arrived in Cambridge. Curious locals looked us over, but they were friendly enough, obviously used to out-of-towners and passing trade.

However, before we could take in the pleasant scenery, the grand buildings with their timber frames and their whitewashed wattle-and-daub walls, we were whisked away to Wickern.

We sat in the back of a rickety cart, pulled by the slowest horse imaginable. No fancy motor-cars had been hired for us, and no train line ran to somewhere so remote. We passed fewer and fewer people on the foggy road, until there was only the horse, the uptight cart-driver, and the ribbiting frogs for company.

Decent bunch of lads, don't get me wrong, but we'd just sat on a train together for some hours. The banter had ran dry. The whiskey, likewise. I wondered whether there'd be a tavern in the little village of Wickern, or whether I'd have to sniff out some bumpkin brewing moonshine.

When we arrived, the first thing that struck me was the mist. It lay like a dense carpet over the village, obscuring the buildings from view. Its probing fingers reached around every corner, pried open every window, and rapped softly at every door.

It was warm, thick, humid fog. I felt like I was chewing it. Was this what it was like all the time out here, I thought? How miserable. How did they keep anything dry? You could see the droplets running down the sides of their sad little buildings.

The cart-driver hopped off and began leading the horse by the bridle. We all hopped out and followed. The houses either side of us, although simple and relatively small, still managed to loom out of the fog in a most unfriendly fashion. There wasn't a man among us who didn't pull his collar up and look furtively from side-to-side.

How big was the village? Well, I wouldn't find out for some days, when the fog would clear and I could see to the end of a street. But I'd be making my hurried exit by then.

Oh, I'm not exaggerating, I couldn't see more than ten feet in front of me... something the Fen Tigers used to their advantage. It was as if they could see straight through it. Thankfully, we wouldn't bump into them just yet.

I jogged up next to the driver, and asked him his name. The horse snorted and shook her head. I stayed well clear. I never was much good with 'em. A cousin of mine took a kick from a horse when we were just kids, I was the one that found him and, well... let's just say I've been wary ever since.

"Sugarlumps, there, there..." the driver said, patting her head.

"Sugarlumps!" I said, laughing. "That's a funny name for a cart-driver."

The man didn't even turn to look at me. Humourless bastard. He simply said, "the name's Everett, sir. And I don't care to learn yours. I hope to be gone tomorrow morning. This place puts the fear in me."

"Well, my man," I said, "why not leave tonight if you're that eager to get away?"

"Sugar needs her rest," he said, "and you don't want to be caught out on the Fens late at night."

"Caught out by what?" I asked incredulously.

"Oh, well Van Buskirk'll tell ya it's these Fen Tigers he's having so much trouble with. For me? It's the lantern-men."

"Tigers? Here? Pull the other one. Sugarlumps here would've been lunch by now. And those 'lantern-men' are nothing but marsh gases. They sure do look spooky though, I'll give you that."

"The Fen Tigers," Everett went on dryly, "are a group of local men who seek to sabotage Van Buskirk's operations. A lot of them will be from this very village. The walls have ears," he said in hushed tones, "so be careful what you say."

"What's their issue?" I asked.

"Folk's livelihoods are at risk. Fishermen, mostly, and simple craftsmen. Mr. Van Buskirk's project will likely take it all away from them. There's something else afoot, though, believe me. The folk here are hiding something, and I'm in no hurry to find out what."

Before I could inquire further, we reached our apparent destination, a building larger than the rest with a small stable leaning-to. It looked sturdier than the others in Wickern, but it was still shabby enough to fit in with the rest of that dump. Everett led Sugarlumps into the stable, and we waited for him to come back out.

Above the doorway of the building, a sign hung limply by its one remaining bracket, depicting a beer mug emblazoned with the words The Stars Align. What a peculiarly grandiose name for an inn in a backwater dump like this, I thought.

"Should have been called The Damp Trousers," I said to the lads, and they snickered.

"The Muddy Boots," said one, "The Toad's Arsehole," said another.

"Shut up," said Everett, leading us to the door, "the walls have ears, remember? You lot go inside and find Van Buskirk. He'll have heard you coming. A deaf elephant would have heard you lot."

"What does Buskirk want, anyway?" I asked. "Details were scant."

"Mr. Van Buskirk," said Everett coldly, "will tell you himself. Can't say I agree with what he's doing, but he pays well."

"Mate," said my colleague Riggs in his heavy Northern accent, "that's our motto."

"Yes, yes. A word of advice, fellas," said Everett gravely, "keep your guard up. These folk stick together, and they'll know exactly why you lot have come. Don't expect a warm welcome."

At this, I smiled, and I said to him: "we never do."

II: The Stars Align

Well, I've told you that the village looked unfriendly enough already. But that was before I'd met any of the locals. Let me tell you, I've been in riots with friendlier atmospheres than the one I found in Wickern's only inn, The Stars Align.

Me and the lads walked in, looked around the room, tried to get our bearings. The room was poorly ventilated. Smoke from the fire made my eyes sting. Absolutely nothing about the decor suggested anything to with stars aligning -- in fact, "decor" is too strong a word for the squalid mess we found ourselves amongst.

A woman stood behind the bar, wiping a beer mug with a cloth that looked dirtier than my socks. And I hadn't changed my socks since Liverpool… still, though, a drink's a drink.

"Pint for me, love," I said jovially, trying to inject some life into the room.

She just stared at me blankly, wiping the glass. It was the weirdest thing. I repeated my request. Still, the staring. I was beginning to think she was deaf, or just a bit thick.

One of the lads behind me, Jock, a big Scottish bastard with violently ginger hair, walked up to the bar. Instinctively, I held out a hand to stop his advance… I knew what that walk meant.

The woman simply looked to her left, toward the main part of the room. A large section of the room was hidden from view, as I soon found out, when about twenty of 'them' emerged from around a corner.

Twenty of the filthiest, most dishevelled, most inbred-looking people I've ever seen in my life shambled towards us. I'm not kidding, these lot were dirtier than scousers. No, no, it's true! And they all brandished glassware at us. One even had a little dagger tucked into his belt. There was no pity in their gaze, no curiosity, only murder.

I hadn't heard a penny drop since walking in. Were they just sitting in silence, the lot of them? Strange, I thought. Were they hiding, or did they just not speak much? What, I supposed, was there to talk about around here?

I heard knuckles and necks crack behind me, even an excited little giggle. The lads were getting ready to do what they did best. They didn't have as much restraint as I did, so I told them to cool it, but the situation was tense.

I'll admit, I didn't know what direction the evening would take.

Right on time, a strange voice called over the room. "Halt! These men are my guests." The accent was foreign. European. A tall, skinny man, in a tattered waistcoat and small glasses, came down the stairs next to the bar.

The men advancing toward us paid the order no heed, until the woman behind the bar waved her hand and said, "errgh, leave 'em. There's no trouble here. Yet."

At her words, the scruffy men stopped their shambling advance. They grumbled and went back to their tables, to sit once again in silence, and stare at each other, or stare at the walls, I don't know... strange folk out there.

"You'll be Van Buskirk, then?" I said.

"Yes, I'll be him. And you are the men I sent for? Come upstairs, please. I have a room more suited for... chatter." He cast a black look over the main room. "I can have the lady bring us drinks, what would you all like?"

At this, my group muttered agreement, and shuffled off up the stairs after him. We sat around a table in a large room upstairs, with a door that we could close behind us, away from prying ears. Halfway down a pint of watery ale, our tongues loosened and we started asking questions.

Well, I'm sure you're dying to know by now. Mr. Van Buskirk's secretive plan to "reclaim some farmland"?

Drain the bloody Fen.

"Sorry, did I just hear you right?"

"Yes," Van Buskirk said, looking down his nose at me through his tiny glasses. "You heard right."

Me and the lads laughed uproariously. "You mad bastard!" we shouted at him, and slapped our knees.

The man was not amused. He informed us, dryly, that he'd had much success doing exactly this kind of thing back in Holland, and that he planned to use much the same method that he did there.

What method, you ask? Well, Van Buskirk was an engineer, as I think I've mentioned. Our madman had a machine.

"I call it D.R.E.A.D.G.E.," he said, "Dreadge for short."

"It's got to be some sort of miracle machine to shift all this water, surely? We're in the middle of a bog, my man," I said incredulously.

"All it has to do to effectively drain Wickern Fen is shift water from flood channels back into the River Ouse. The machine is actually a great deal more advanced than that. It's something of a pet project of mine... but I digress."

"Oh yeah?" asked Riggs, "what else does it do?"

"It's full name is the Dredging Raising Excavating Aqueous-Draining Grave Exhumer."

"Grave Exhumer!?" I sputtered. "What have you brought us here for, Van Buskirk? We're not into all that. We're just a bit of muscle for when things get hairy. Grave robbing isn't our style."

A few of the men shrugged as if to say, "it didn't bother them," "they might have done that kind of thing already," and "this very much was their style if the money was right." I frowned at them, and they returned to their pints.

"Yes, well," said Van Buskirk, "don't worry. I simply aim to drain the Fen. These vast tracts will later be used as arable farmland. Your job is to stop the locals disrupting me, and that's it. I think you'll agree that the pay is generous."

"First time I've ever said this, but it's too generous. To stop a bunch of malnourished freaks interfering with one machine? Is that who you're scared of, those lot downstairs? I had to stop Jock snapping them all in two."

"Aye, and I only didnae cause I've no been paid yet," Jock said. Always was a man of few words, Jock.

"Yes, well," Van Buskirk went on, "I can't understand what your friend is saying, but I'm glad he held himself back. The reception is… lukewarm, at best, in this inn, but it is the only inn for many miles around.

"It is fortunate that my fellow engineers and I can stay somewhere so close to the drainage site. The very moment you lift a finger against the locals, is the moment that this privilege ends for us all."

"Aren't we here to cave their heads in?" asked Riggs.

Van Buskirk raised an eyebrow. "Well, hopefully it won't come to that, but the group calling themselves the Fen Tigers are a great deal more ferocious than that rabble downstairs."

He went on to describe the troubles he'd been having. First, surveying equipment would disappear, or engine parts would go missing. Food would be stolen, shoes and waders would be slit through the soles and rendered useless.

Every step of the way, from surveying, to bringing his engineers and his infernal machine here, to setting up the machine itself, had taken him ten times longer than it should have.

These activists had even switched some of the signposts around, leading his surveyors astray and causing a fortnight's worth of maps to be scrapped. I'll admit, that one gave us a chuckle. Very mischievous.

Van Buskirk found it less funny. "That was a very costly act of mischief, and it didn't stop there," he said. "Soon, our equipment was smashed. They attacked us more brazenly. Big, wiry men, not like the ones downstairs."

His eyes grew wide and his speech had grown more frantic. "I don't know where they go, I don't know where they sleep. It's like they just… emerge, out of the mist, and then disappear back into it."

"Well," I said, "they sound annoying, but not so terrible. Nothing we can't handle."

Van Buskirk leaned over the table, and gestured for us to lean in. He said in a low, conspiratorial voice, "about a week ago, one of my engineers disappeared. I immediately put in the notice for you men, fearing the worst."

"He still hasn't turned up?"

Van Buskirk held a finger up to his lips. "The locals don't know that we know yet. We found him."

"Alive?"

He shook his head. "Mangled."

This raised a few eyebrows. Just then, the door opened.

That grizzled landlady was there, offering us more drinks. Bollocks, I remember thinking, good hospitality all of a sudden? She was trying to listen in. She certainly overstayed her welcome, slowly collecting glasses while we sat there in stony silence.

After she'd left, Van Buskirk closed the door behind her and shook his head.

Riggs piped up then. "Thing that's bothering me," he said, "is why they let you stay 'ere. If they're willing to 'mangle' one of your men, why don't they just 'mangle' you in your sleep? Problem solved."

In response, Van Buskirk rubbed his thumb and forefingers together. "They can't turn down the coin I'm offering. Every day they tell me the room rates have increased, or the food and drink is more expensive now due to ingredient shortages or missed deliveries. And I have had no choice but to pay up."

"Hah! Good racket. We're in the wrong game," I said.

"Indeed. The sooner I can complete my work, the better, but for them, the longer they can bleed me dry, the better… and time is of the essence," Van Buskirk muttered, "the stars are aligning, after all…"

"What's that?"

"Oh, nothing. Ignore me."

I knew something was up here, but I didn't want to press him too hard. We still hadn't seen any coin yet, remember. It's all too easy to talk yourself out of a wage packet… that's a lesson you only need to learn once.

"Tell me more about this fella who turned up dead, then," I said. "How mangled are we talking?"

"Well…"

Listen, I'll do you a favour. I won't repeat everything he told me. But it certainly made me think twice about those Fen Tigers. Van Buskirk span us a gruesome yarn. It turned our stomachs. We were hard-faced blokes, used to a scrap, but we weren't used to things like this.

"And the worst thing," he said, almost whispering, "he was propped up with one finger pointing toward the centre of Wickern Fen. They'd hammered a stake right through the middle of his body to keep him there in the mud, knee-deep, and another one through the wrist to hold up the pointing hand. And Lord only knows where the poor fellow's head is."

A chorus of muttering arose around the table.

"Either bobbing about in the Fen somewhere, or these freaks have taken it for some reason," I said, in disgust.

"We don't know yet. He was hard to find in all that fog. We only found him because we found the torn bloody strips of his robe floating around in the water nearby."

"Hang on," Jock butted in, "his robe? Whit kind of engineer wears a robe?"

Van Buskirk coughed. "Slip of the tongue. His coat. Strips of his coat."

The lads looked at each other uneasily over the table. An awkward silence fell.

"I think it's time for me to retire, anyway, gentlemen," Van Buskirk said. He looked around the table. "I don't think I'll have much luck telling men like you not to drink too much, but we will be leaving at dawn tomorrow for the Fen. Prepare accordingly."

At this, he slunk off to bed. We had one more drink, and tried to have a bit of a laugh, but there was an atmosphere that was hard to shake off. We'd just heard about a man butchered and staked in a desolate bog, after all… every single one of us was wondering whether that would be our own fate.

It should have been a case for the police, really, but for whatever reason, Van Buskirk didn't want to involve the authorities. Or, I thought at the time, his patrons didn't.

We went to bed shortly afterwards. Due to the modest size of the inn, we were two-to-a-room, but this wasn't so bad. We'd slept in worse conditions, for sure, although none quite so damp. Water dripped down the wooden walls of the rooms, creeping fingers of moisture that made the bedclothes cold and clammy.

By far the worst part of the story, though, was that I'd drawn the short straw. I was sharing with Jock. The smell that man could produce, after beer and a good meal, was legendary. A fate even worse than the one suffered by Van Buskirk's 'fellow engineer' out in the bog, I thought, as I struggled to sleep through the Scotchman's snoring.

III: The Fen Tigers

We met outside the inn in the morning, when the fog was just beginning to light up. I say that because there was no 'sunrise' to speak of, it was simply that the sky viewed through the fog became lighter than it was at night time.

No, there was no sun in the sky.

I mean, it was probably up there, but I had no idea where it was. I couldn't feel its warmth, that's for sure. I hadn't felt it since entering that cursed Fen. The fog buried us and smothered us… entombed us. We couldn't breathe properly, as though we were buried under sand, but at the same time, we couldn't get warm or dry.

Van Buskirk led us out of the village, deep into Wickern Fen. We barely said a word along the way. Whether we were hung over, poorly rested, or just uneasy, I can't say. Most likely, we were a little of all three.

We were on foot. I'm averse to horse-riding, as I've said, but I'd have ridden one gladly through that terrain. The road back to Cambridge was fairly well set, but we were going in almost the opposite direction.

Out this way, the road melted into mud a few minutes outside of the village. Almost deafening us was the constant cacophony made by nesting birds and croaking frogs and toads, and the wind rushing through the reeds.

All we had to guide us was Van Buskirk, with a wooden torch aflame in his hand, trudging through the mud. He'd given us leather waders before we left Wickern, and before we were five minutes away from The Stars Align, we were glad to have them.

We walked thigh-deep through muddy water, and at different times, each of us fell flat on our faces and had to be pulled back up to the surface by our colleagues. It was funny the first few times, but a whole hour in? Not so much. We were soaked, our waders were waterlogged, and we were losing our patience.

Van Buskirk had no such trouble. Obviously he was much more used to this route than we were. He had a compass which pointed East-Southeast.

I tried to make a note of any landmarks, just in case I needed to make my way back by myself, but I soon found out that there were no landmarks at all.

Could I remember that particular rock? That particular patch of reeds? That particular nest of bitterns? How could I, when we'd passed ten nests of bitterns, and would pass a good deal more before we reached our destination?

Our destination, as it happened, loomed out of the mist just as I was starting to think Mr. Van Buskirk was taking the piss out of us.

A rather large barn, about the size of The Stars Align inn but more simple and more rectangular, appeared through the fog as though it had grown organically out of the water. The mist had not let up a single inch, and it was no easier to see ten feet away than it was in the village.

There were figures in high-collared coats lurking ominously around the barn, some of them holding flaming torches themselves. I could barely make out their faces. Lord knows where they'd slept -- surely not in that barn, I thought. It didn't even have doors.

The front of the barn was wide open to the elements -- in fact, a large tract of water seemed to lead directly into it. It would soon become apparent that this was exactly where they'd intended to house that infernal machine, Dreadge, as just nearby the Fen breached the bank of the River Ouse.

Van Buskirk disappeared inside of the barn, while we watched from outside, cold and wet. The men standing guard around it looked at us with disdain. The coats they wore were gigantic, over-sized, but maybe that's just what you had to wear out here to keep warm and dry, I told myself.

I walked up to one of them and asked for a cigarette. I had a few on me, and so did the lads, but they were sodden after our falls into the bog. They would take some time to dry out.

These men looked at us pitilessly, as though we were dirt. We were used to cold receptions, but these lot were different to the Fenmen in the inn. They didn't want to kill us, they just looked at us like we were piles of shite that they had stepped in.

I remember frowning. Who did they think they were? We were working together, yes, and for good pay. But there's only so far you can push a man. Men like Jock and Riggs had throttled people over less... and men like me had spirited them away from the police afterwards.

One of Van Buskirk's men craned his neck up above his collar and said to us, in thick Dutch, something like, "vers vlees voor her moeras." His men within earshot laughed. Nasty, hacking laughs they were, as though they were full of phlegm. Obviously they spent a lot of time out in the swamp.

Not one of us spoke Dutch, or a single word of anything apart from our native English, although we'd had arguments over whether Jock spoke English or something entirely different...

Anyway, these lot were Dutchmen that Van Buskirk had brought over to England. Whether they actually couldn't speak English, or whether they were just excluding us, I never found out. But they were arseholes, I know that much. We never got a single cigarette, or an ounce of respect, from those Dutchmen out in the bog.

I managed to walk up to the barn and take a look inside.

What I saw confused me at the time; I saw a waterwheel; I saw an engine; I saw an astrolabe; I saw a complex system of pulleys, weights and counterweights. The thing sprawled out in all directions, looking a great deal more arcane and esoteric than a dredging device had any right to look.

What the hell was this thing, I remember thinking, surely all it needed to do was push water with the waterwheel? What were all the other things for? As my eyes adjusted to the gloom in the barn, I made out symbols carved into the wooden parts and the metal frame of the machine.

Symbols I didn't recognise. Symbols I didn't like.

Just as I began to turn my nose up at what I saw within the barn, a few of Van Buskirk's silent guardsmen closed in on my position, blocking my view.

I waded back to my men, shaking my head. "I don't like this much," I said.

"Naw," said Jock, "me neither."

"We supposed to be protecting this, then?" asked Riggs. "I can't even see the other side of that bloody barn through the fog, never mind these 'Tigers' Van B. was on about."

Right on cue, we heard splashing nearby. Could have been a hunting heron, I thought, or a short-eared owl preying on a yellow wagtail.

That was, at least, until I heard a scream from a few feet away. A human scream, not the scream of some hapless fenland bird.

I whirled around and drew my pocket knife, as did the other lads, but my feet were unsteady in the mud beneath the water. It was hard to lift a foot out of the bog. Putting a foot back down knocked my balance skew-whiff. My legs were jelly.

We looked around frantically. We saw, with dismay, that our man Blakey was floating face-down in the water, trails of deep red claret reaching out from him in all directions. Blakey had faced down hordes of the great unwashed with nary a scratch ever applied to his handsome visage, yet there he was, bobbing sad and limp in the swamp.

We lashed out, stabbing blindly, striking with torch and knife and fist and club, yet our weapons connected with nothing. The mist dispersed in front of us, and reformed moments afterwards, as though mocking our impotence.

We couldn't see hide nor hair of the attacker that had laid Blakey low. We turned him around to assess the damage and saw two clean, but very deep and deliberate cuts. One in the back of the knee, obviously the one that drew the scream, and one deep into the throat, which would have seen him off moments later.

We huddled together instinctively, forming a circle with our backs together and our weapons outstretched. We could see nothing. No attackers. Suddenly, the threat posed by these Fen Tigers became much more real to me. These men obviously knew the geography, and the swampy terrain, so much better than we did. What chance did we stand against them?

Van Buskirk's men, similarly, drew themselves together, although they formed a double-line in front of the open door of the barn. I remember thinking, then, why the hell does that machine need an astrolabe!?

Obviously it had taken me a few minutes to process what I saw in there. I could think of no good reason why this thing would need to track the stars above our heads. Granted, we couldn't see the stars for the fog, but why did Van Burskirk need to know exactly how they were arranged in the sky above our location?

I was a great deal more suspicious of him from that moment on. He'd told us that this machine could do more than push water from place to place, but not why it would need to. He was only here to 'drain the Fen', right?

Now that one of my men was lying dead in the water, I resolved to ask him what Dreadge did and why. I was sure that the Fen Tigers knew, and that was why they were willing to kill any intruders.

Van Buskirk came out of the barn, then, torch held high. He waded out in front of his Dutch compatriots and shouted above the din of the nesting birds: "Fen Tigers! Disperse! You cannot possibly hope to win against this many men! We will do what we are here to do, no more, and no less!"

At this, I heard something from out in the fog. A quick whooshing sound. Van Buskirk ducked, and the Dutchman behind him took a jagged stone to the gullet, and fell gurgling into the bog-water. They'd obviously thrown something with a crude sling of some sort… the projectile was too quick and too accurate to have been thrown by hand.

How could they be that accurate in the fog, I thought… I couldn't see the man throwing it, so how could he see Van Buskirk? Maybe they were so adept at navigating this foggy Fenland that they knew where somebody was just by the sound of their voice.

At least, that's how I reasoned with myself at the time. If there was something supernatural spurring them on, well, then I wanted to escape as soon as possible back to the cities, where things made more sense.

Van Buskirk's Dutchmen roared, and a few of them drew blades. The ones at the front ran out into the fog together, ready to do battle with whatever they came across.

"Is that how it is," I said to the lads, "happy to avenge their own, but not one of ours…"

I received some growling responses, which suggested to me that nobody had taken the loss of Blakey lightly.

Van Buskirk waded quickly toward us and said, "follow me back to Wickern, gentlemen. I have done what I needed to do."

"What the hell did you need to do," I shouted, "one of our men is dead!"

"Yes, well," he said, "his pay will be split out amongst the rest of you." The way he said it was cold, unfeeling, as though he held the death of a man in no more regard than the death of a midge. I was seething, but a few of the lads made pleased little grunting noises, as though they were happy with this arrangement.

Rather than cause a fall-out between us all in the middle of the swamp, with the Tigers presumably lurking in the mist, I deigned to follow Van Buskirk without any more argument. I did ask him again about what he was doing, though.

"Just making some adjustments to the astrolabe," he answered.

"The astrolabe? A man died for that!" I shouted.

"Two men, actually. One of mine went down too."

"Oh, and that makes things better, does it?"

"No," Van Buskirk said, "it changes nothing."

I didn't know how to reply.

I merely trudged through the Fen, my men strung out behind me in a long line, following Van Buskirk's torch.

I thought then on the astrolabe... something about it seriously bothered me. It was huge, you know. Not like a pocket one you might find in a gift shop.

No, this thing was the same size as the waterwheel on the side of Dreadge... it was attached to the opposite side of the machine, and ran counter-clockwise to the clockwise motion of the wheel as it took up water and passed it to a wooden viaduct above.

Adjustments to the astrolabe? He took us all the way out there for that? It still bothers me now. Dreadge was a powerful and mysterious machine, to be sure, but just how far did its powers stretch? What exactly did it have control over?

I was no engineer, but that was when I started to wonder: what forces could this machine manipulate? What, if one knew enough about mathematics and science and astrology, were the limits of this occult kind of engineering?

We got back to Wickern. We stood outside of The Stars Align, at around sunset, as the sky began to dim. I looked at our group and counted eight of us, including myself... Hutchie hadn't made it back. I shouted, I raged at the rest of the men, how the fuck did nobody notice he was gone?

"He was at the back," Riggs answered matter-of-factly.

I shook my head. We'd have to watch ourselves in this Fen, I thought. In our entire careers, we had never lost a man, except to marriage or to syphilis. Now we'd lost two. If I could get my hands on those bastards, I'd throttle every one of them myself.

Van Buskirk told us that there was now one less man for our pay to be shared amongst. Jock and I looked at each other uneasily, while the rest of the men shrugged and went inside the inn. I stayed outside with Jock, and Van Buskirk tried to go inside the building himself, but we blocked his path.

"This is wrong, mate," I said, "I've just lost two good friends and all you can talk about is money. What the hell is going on? What have you got that horrible machine doing?"

Van Buskirk adjusted his glasses, and said to us, "for you two, double-pay."

Jock said, "you're jokin'."

"The situation is far too grave, and far too urgent, for me to tell jokes," Van Buskirk said. From beneath his shirt, he pulled out a leather pouch, and from that pouch he peeled ten one-pound notes. He gave us five each.

"My gift to you," he said, "but keep it quiet. There's plenty more where that came from. Now, why don't I buy you boys a drink?"

Dazzled, we followed him inside. A great many drinks were had, and a great many toasts to our fallen comrades Blakey and Hutchie, and I'll be honest with you: the details of that evening are regrettably rather obscured in my memory.

I learned something about myself that night, though. No matter who you are, a comrade's memory can be bought away... for some, it might cost more than for others, but as my agent in London is fond of saying, every man has his price.

IV: Disturbance

I can't remember going to bed, but I can sure as hell remember waking up. I'd never woken up with my heart hammering so heavily in my ears before... but I've woken up that way plenty of times since.

We stayed up much of that night, drinking. Later on, as the alcohol kicked in, there was singing and laughing, but I can't remember the specifics. It took a lot of drink for us to forget the events in the Fen.

Anyway, at some point, we retired to bed. I was still sharing a room with Jock, so I was used to strange sounds in the night. The kind of sounds that can shake a man to his core and keep him awake, terrified and struggling for breath.

However, on that night, I heard something that scared me even more than Jock's rotten arsepipe: the door-handle rattled and the door creaked open.

I leapt out of bed, in my underwear, ready to face whoever had crept into my room this late. After what I'd just seen in the Fen, I'd kept a pocket knife under my pillow, and I'd fallen asleep with my hand gripping the handle tightly. I lashed out with it as I rose.

I heard a yelp in the darkness, and a man scrambled out of my room. I chased the intruder all the way down the corridor, all the way down the stairs, and out into the muddy lane which lay outside The Stars Align.

As I could see that my prey would soon melt into the mist, I thought 'to hell with it', and threw my knife at his back.

I heard a scream, and, not believing my luck, it took a moment before I sprang to action and ran after him. I hollered for my companions, just to be sure that I wasn't killed by this man's comrades. I heard everyone clambering down the stairs inside the inn, shouting incoherently.

I jumped on the prone body I found on the floor, and turned him around to face me. He was big and burly, unnaturally so for a man out here in the Fens. He was unclean and unshaven, but he had a noble face and a strong jaw. He looked at me with deep blue eyes that contained more sadness than desperation or anger.

"You don't know what that Van Buskirk's up to," the man said in his thick accent. He coughed up blood; obviously the dagger in his back hadn't proved too beneficial for his health.

He reached around and pulled it out, groaning as he did so. I was wary, but the man looked weak now, and it didn't seem as though he was trying to stab me with it.

"Yeah," I said, panting, "no idea. Tell me?"

He wouldn't tell me.

Fearing that he was on death's door, I asked him whether he

was one of these Fen Tigers, asked him about his fellow warriors, even offered him medical help and safe passage if he imparted any knowledge on how to fight them, or even just to find them.

I had no intention of following through on my promises, but he couldn't have known that.

Regardless, he raised the knife that I'd thrown, the one that he'd pulled out of his own back. He was too weak to be a threat, but all the same, I gripped his wrist with both hands and steered his hand away from me. My men, by now stood around us in a big circle, watched with keen interest.

Now, you might not believe this next part. But why would I lie? Believe me, I take no pleasure in imparting the following memory: the man wasn't fighting against me. In fact, he used my own strength to hasten his aim: using his nimble fingers, he manipulated the knife so that the point was facing toward himself.

He opened his mouth. He thrust downward with the knife, and at the same time, thrust upward with his neck and head. The knife pierced the back of his throat with a hideous noise, and the man turned his own wrist so savagely that he sputtered blood all over me.

There was no saving him, so I didn't try. He was dead in less than ten seconds. My men, having watched the whole grisly escapade, bellowed and groaned in disgust.

They retreated back inside upon seeing that it was over. Obviously, they feared that this dead man's fellow Tigers were lurking in the midnight mist just outside the inn. They very likely were, so I followed them in swiftly.

Jock, having finally risen from his slumber, came downstairs with a candle in his hand. He lit a few of the other candles set into the walls. I counted the men: six of us.

My heart sank.

"You have to be fucking kidding me!" I shouted as I ran up the stairs, leaping them three at a time, and booted open every bedroom door.

Surely enough, there was Riggs and his roommate Rugely in

one of the rooms, lying still in their beds. Their pillows and sheets were darkly stained. Their throats had been cut in the night. They'd gone without the smallest sign of a struggle.

Jock and I were obviously next on the chopping block. Luckily I can't sleep too well whenever I'm within five feet of that big ginger bastard.

Predictably, the commotion had risen the entire inn. The landlady, our ever-pleasant bartender, stood at the bottom of the stairs, saying nothing, her mad hair reaching out in all directions like straw from a scarecrow.

We could hear more voices from outside, not threatening ones, but the voices of curious village-folk coming to see what the fuss was about.

Every single one of the locals pleaded ignorance, of course, but at this point I was too paranoid to believe them. I fully believed they had come out to murder us outright, or, failing that, murder us in "self-defence" if we threatened the landlady.

As far as I was concerned, this had been allowed to happen, the Fen Tigers were allowed in and now my good pals Riggs and Rugely were both dead in their beds. But now, with only six of us left, and twenty villagers, and god-knows-how-many of those Fen Tigers lurking outside, I decided to keep quiet and calm.

I wanted out of here, fast, but Everett and Sugarlumps hadn't returned to town yet. We hadn't a hope in Hell's chance of getting out of the Fen alive walking, even if we stuck to the road to Cambridge. The Fen Tigers would harry us from the mist on either side, and we'd die there, bleeding into the bog.

That was the point when we became utterly demoralised. The point when we became completely terrified of the Fen Tigers. Whatever they were trying to defend, I thought, was obviously well worth defending, and I was sorry that I ever got in their way.

Van Buskirk came downstairs, and tried to calm us down. He assured us that there would be no trip to the barn this morning, as Dreadge had ran into some complications. Tomorrow, however, was the 'big day', the day he expected the main drainage of

Wickern Fen to commence. On that day, we would be required.

"Yeah? Let me guess," I said, with a hot temper, "it's worth it because there's only six to split the pay amongst now?"

"Well," Van Buskirk said, "yes. How can you argue with that? The job's almost over, and you've all increased your pay significantly. Hold out until the end, and who knows how much you'll earn."

Even the greediest of my men couldn't be enthusiastic about this prospect. Jock looked less amused than ever. To my knowledge, that man has never smiled, so you must understand how grave this reaction was. We said nothing, and simply looked at Van Buskirk with grim expressions.

"I'm going out to make some very minor adjustments to Dreadge today," he said, "I do not require an escort this time. They won't know I've left if I leave now."

"I don't care if you 'require an escort' or not," I growled, "you could turn up dead tomorrow for all I care. Get us out of this accursed place. Keep your bloody money."

"Everett will be back soon enough with his cart, and you can all leave. Our job will be done by then. And you will get to keep your bloody money."

"What do we do today, then, sit here and get murdered?"

Van Buskirk made his way toward the door. "Gentlemen," he said, "I would recommend resting up today. Sit in the upstairs room where we talked upon your arrival, it is comfortable enough." He leaned in, and said under his breath, "watch the door and the windows. Keep your wits about you."

At this, he dived out of the door, carrying no torch. It was uncanny, the way he could slip through boggy wetland without making a noise. We splashed around like fools whenever we were out in it, but Van Buskirk was barely detectable.

All too fitting for a sneaky, lying little bastard like him, I thought bitterly, as we piled into the upstairs room and tried not to think about our friends lying cold and dead in their bedroom just down the corridor.

Jock grumbled to me, out of earshot of the others, "what woulda happened if we got oor throats cut, eh? Double-pay forgotten about, that's what."

I hadn't thought of that. Van Buskirk had melted into the night by this point, and all too well, because if I'd found him in that moment, I'd have squeezed the eyeballs out of his skull.

V: Hunted

We holed up in that large upstairs room for the rest of the night, refusing to open the door to anybody who knocked. Nothing, as yet, had turned violent. We had a chair wedged up against the door handle in case anybody tried to enter. Nobody did.

The small square window at the back of the room showed that daylight had come. With it, a miserable drizzling rain came tapping against the pane.

Jock paced back and forth. I drummed my fingers on the table, and the rest of the lads fidgeted too. One lad, Coggins, from Devon way, chain-smoked every single cigarette in our possession. We chastised him, but he looked at us with violence in his eyes, like a cornered beast.

The last thing we needed was to fight amongst ourselves, and do the Fen Tigers' job for them, so we let him be.

This way, we passed some of the sweatiest, most tense, most frustrating hours of our lives.

Eventually we agreed to poke our head out and see if anything was occurring. Quietly, we drew our knives and opened the door, only to find that nobody was there, but that some food had been left on a tray for us on the floor. Stale bread and some fried potatoes and onions.

We were hungry, but not one of us touched that food.

We sneaked out into our bedrooms and raided them for supplies, our tinned emergency rations that we carried in our little bags. I took Riggs and Rugely's from their room.

I'll always remember the way their cold, dead eyes stared outward in panic, their slack jaws drooling onto their pillows... and the great gashes where their necks used to connect smoothly to their heads. Their wounds were turning black and crusty.

I closed their eyes and slunk back to the large room.

We didn't talk much. The rain picked up and battered at the window.

I had an odd thought then, that Van Buskirk and his strange machine might have something to do with the change in the weather, but I soon dispelled that notion as being too daft. The rain didn't clear the fog, anyway, that's for sure. I still couldn't see much of anything out of that window.

As the hours passed toward late afternoon, and we were beginning to doze in our chairs, we heard more commotion. We sprang to action. We barricaded the door. We drew knives, batons, anything we had to hand. Jock wielded the fire poker. We faced the door in anticipation…

Lots of shouting voices. More than ten men ran straight past our little room. We looked at each other, confused.

"The hell are they doing?" Jock asked.

I held a finger up to my lips, and listened keenly at the door. The men appeared to be going up one further floor, to the garret where Van Buskirk slept and kept his office, his little base of operations.

I heard a door handle rattle, and then the door banged repeatedly against the frame. In moments, there was an almighty crash and the sound of something hitting the floor.

"They've broken into Van Buskirk's room," I said through gritted teeth, "they must think he's still here."

"So we're not the targets, then?" asked Coggins.

"Not while we're awake and expecting them, I'll bet," I said, "that's not their style, is it? They're obviously scared of a fair fight."

"Then let's go and give them wan, for fuck's sake!" said Jock. His voice always rose in pitch when he was agitated. I could tell he was spoiling for a fight. "We'll catch wan o' they freaks and ask him what's gon' on!"

"You know, that's not a bad idea," I said, "catch the ambushers by surprise."

Before we could act, however, we heard a tumbling from above, and a great many disappointed voices. They immediately ran down the stairs and approached our doorway.

Wordlessly, I held some fingers up for the lads: four fingers, three fingers, two, one…

Jock shoulder-barged our barricade out of the way, and I leapt out of the door. The last man in their little party looked back in shock. He was at the top of the stairs to the main bar room, just about to make his way down.

While he was still gawping, I dived onto his back and sent us both tumbling down the stairs. I rolled around on the floor of the inn with him, trading blows, trying to pin him down, but he was a wiry one, he was nimble, and he fought like a caged animal… well, a caged Tiger.

My men followed, and just as I saw a few of the Fen Tigers approach me with blades, Jock leapt over us on the floor and skewered one of them through the eye with his poker as he landed. He let out a mighty roar, and sent the rest of the Tigers scattering away.

Having successfully restrained my man, with a little help from Coggins and the other three, we bundled him back upstairs and holed up in the big room behind our barricaded door. He still bit and scratched us like a lunatic, so Jock clobbered him in the temple, and then he was out for the count.

Curiously, I thought, the bottom floor of the inn was empty. Not even the landlady was there. Why was that? Usually this place was chock-full of the local down-and-outs, drowning their lives away in ale. The place was stinking of booze, as though they'd spilled all the strong spirits and not cleaned up.

We tied this man to a chair upstairs, anyway. It took an hour or so until he woke up, and we began our interrogation. I was never much good at this kind of thing. I'm too good-natured, you see. A bit of a softy.

That's why we left it to Jock.

The large, angry, sweaty, ginger-bearded Scot waved his poker around in our man's face… it was still covered with a good deal of the gooey remnants of its last victim's head. Looking at this gruesome implement made me feel ill. I'm sure the man in the chair felt likewise.

I turned away. I didn't want to see what was about to happen -- this was one of the more unpleasant parts of jobs like ours -- sometimes people needed a little persuasion to act how they were supposed to act. A tooth here, a nail there.

Before any of that, though, miraculously, our man spoke.

"Stop waving that thing in my face, for God's sake! I'll talk! In fact, I must tell you!"

"Tell us what," I asked. I turned to face the man and saw genuine urgency in his eyes.

"Don't you know what that Van Buskirk is doing?"

"Draining the fen. I understand you lot aren't happy about this. But we're not happy about our four dead colleagues."

"Look, needs must," he said, in his thick Fenland accent, "we tried to be gentle, but that Van Buskirk's incorrigible. Stronger messages needed to be sent."

I looked at him pitilessly. That was no excuse to kill my friends, or so I thought at the time.

He went on, "go and search his room! There's more to this than just draining the Fen… why do you think he's so hell-bent on doing it? Why do you think he's pouring so much money into it? He's poured hundreds, thousands of pounds into this!"

Letting the man catch his breath, I mulled over what he'd said. "It won't be him pouring money in, will it," I said, "it'll be the government or some such. Some fat-cat bankrolling him, wanting the land."

"No! It's all his own money! He doesn't care about the land! He's nearly bankrupted himself paying for his machine and for his enforcers… Do you think you're the first lot of brutes we've put down?"

I'd suspected as much, to be honest. That we weren't the first lot of men to die out here in this godforsaken bog for the sake of Dreadge. But I had more questions.

"Why," I said deliberately, "would he pour so much of his own money and effort into draining this hell-hole, then?"

"I- I can't say," the man said, looking frightened. I winced as the back of Jock's hand immediately shot out and struck the man on the cheek. The grisly poker made a re-appearance, and the man began to wail.

"Why?" I repeated.

"Just go up to his office and see for yourself! There's something beneath... beneath the bog... he's trying to pull it up. He's trying to dredge it..." the man gibbered now, eyes wild, "and we tried to stop him, we did, we tried to keep it hidden, our folk, for as long as history goes back, our folk have been here and we've always kept it hidden--"

"Kept WHAT hidden!" I roared.

"Go upstairs and see! Read his notes! I've never seen it, have I!? It's hidden! Beneath the bog!"

I found his logic hard to argue with, but still, I knew this man was evading me.

I knelt down to his level. "You are going to die in this chair if you don't tell me what is under that bog," I growled. Jock waved the poker menacingly.

"I... I can't describe it. Nobody can. It eludes description. It's... cosmic, it's beyond our world. Normally, it wouldn't even be there, but when... when the stars align... when the stars align it'll be there. And strangers should stay away."

I shook my head at him. This wasn't good enough, but it was certainly intriguing.

He began sobbing in the chair. "You have to stop him," he said, "you have to stop him dredging that bog. It won't just be the end of Wickern Fen. It'll be the end of everything."

Rather than waste precious time on this crying wreck of a man, I grabbed a couple of the lads and went up to search Van Buskirk's garret.

What we found up there... well. Hard to describe. I found absolutely nothing that I expected to find in an engineer's office, that's for certain. With the rain pounding against the thin roof, just inches above our heads, we poked around by candlelight.

There were no diagrams, no schematics, no detailed plans, no, nothing of the sort...

There were maps of the Fen, but large portions of them had red X's drawn through them, as though he had been trying to narrow down a specific location. A large black circle was drawn around a circular patch of the bog, just Southeast of Wickern. I realised this would have been we were yesterday, where Dreadge was located.

Around the circle on the map were drawn horrible little symbols, the same kind of symbols that I'd seen carved into the wood on the machine. In fact, we found reams of these symbols. They were on maps, on star-charts, carved into the desk, and doodled into the margins of note-books.

I flipped through his books, but they were all in Dutch. Might as well have been more of the same arcane symbols to me, I couldn't read a word... but what I found underneath that stack of notebooks still makes me shudder to think about.

A vast, dusty tome. It looked old, so old that it should have been crumbling away to nothing, but it was curiously well-preserved. I couldn't make out the title, as it was written in more of those strange symbols, although it was embossed in gold lettering against the black binding.

That was when I realised the symbols formed some kind of alphabet.

The more I stared at them, the more I became mesmerised... seeing them laid out like that, as text, was deeply absorbing. My mind began to wander, I began to think of the stars, and how much I missed seeing them twinkle in the sky... I yearned to return to them one day. To leave my earthly form behind and rejoin my brothers in the sky.

Such an odd thought had never entered my mind before, and I swear, it was those dodgy symbols, even though you can't read them, they do something funny to your head, something in your mind understands them, regardless of whether you know what they mean.

My fingers crept to the corner of the cover, and I wanted so desperately to lift it and see more, but at that moment, I heard creaking upon the garret steps.

"Gentlemen."

I looked up. It was Van Buskirk.

"You," I said, "have a lot to answer for."

"As do you," he said, promptly. "I'd call this an invasion of privacy, wouldn't you?"

"It wasn't us that turned over your office," I said irritably, "it was the bloody Tigers. We've got one tied up downstairs. You're lucky you weren't here when they came in -- they meant murder."

"Is that right," he muttered under his breath, "very brave of them. They must have ran out of the need for my money. That or they've noticed the stars."

He observed my fingers on his book. They were still there, as though the thing had a magnetic pull. I met his gaze. I wasn't about to back down. I wanted answers.

"Well, since the cat's out of the bag, so to speak," he said, "yes, there's more to this operation. There's something under this bog that I'm very interested in uncovering, as are my friends out there in the barn with my dear Dreadge."

"What?" I growled. I was about done with this charade.

"To tell you the truth, I'm not entirely sure. But whatever it is, it is the culmination of years of study. Years of hunting. All the secret societies of the world could not dream of what's beneath Wickern Fen... something older than humanity itself." He sounded wistful.

I knew he was insane, but my morbid curiosity was piqued. "The man we have downstairs says it'll be the end of everything," I said.

"Your man downstairs is an ignorant fool who has never left the desolate swamp he grew up in. Do you think that might have something to do with his belief in such superstitions?"

I shrugged. I was uneasy, but the man was persuasive, I'll give him that.

"Would you let such ignorance stand in the way of scientific progress? Such deep knowledge of the world and its history? This could be the biggest discovery there has ever been. And you'll be there to witness it."

"And I'll be unimaginably wealthy, won't I, Van Buskirk? You'll be most generous with your newfound fame and riches."

He smiled a hideous smile. The smile of a man that knows they've hooked me into their plan with nothing but my own greed as bait... judge me all you want. It was a smile I was used to seeing. Usually on the face of my agent.

Suddenly, there were sounds from below. Smashed windows. A hot whoomph.

Moments later, Jock bellowed up the stairs, "they've set the fuckin' place on fire! Get oot, pronto!"

Even Van Buskirk looked worried at this. He took one last panicked look around his room, and his eyes fixed longingly on the book.

"Too heavy," he sighed. "It has served its purpose, anyway."

He walked quickly over to his wardrobe, and pulled out a robe. I watched in fascination, frozen despite the urgency of the situation. The robe was black, and had those horrid symbols stitched into the hood. He pulled it on, and grabbed a small leather bag from the floor of the wardrobe.

He caught me looking, jaw agape, and said, "look, there's a lot about this operation that you don't understand."

"I'll say," I muttered, and we made our way down the stairs. Jock and the other lads were coming up the other way. "Too hot doon there," he shouted, "they must have doused the entire bar in spirits. There'll be more bottles -- the whole thing's gonnae blow!"

Surely enough, we heard bottles bursting below. We crowded into the garret, six of us and Van Buskirk. Without wasting any more time, Jock picked the chair from behind the desk and threw it through the garret window.

"Gonnae have to jump, lads," he said gravely. "The ground's soft enough. It's a swamp. And it's rainin." Even he didn't sound fully convinced.

Still, though, three storeys doesn't seem all that high when you're in a burning building. Five of my group jumped, one after the other, and we landed with a heavy thud in the mud below. Van Buskirk simply... landed next to us, impossibly gracefully, in absolute silence.

Even now, there is a lot that I do not understand about that man. He'd dedicated his time to things that nobody should know, and that's about all I can say.

I could hear the hooting and hollering of the villagers from the other side of the inn. It wouldn't be long until they found out how we'd escaped. Doubtless, the silent Fen Tigers would have been prowling through the reeds toward us too. Van Buskirk began to lead us off into the marsh, to Dreadge, but Jock was still up in the garret.

With a heavy heart, I looked up. Such a big man, full of muscle and carrying a great deal of whisky-weight, was not well-suited to falling from height. With all the grace of a lead balloon on fire, he plummeted to earth. I heard a sickening snap as he hit the floor.

He howled in pain, and I wanted to help him, but I knew I'd never be able to drag that big old bastard through miles of marshland. His shouting had drawn attention, and before long, they were on him, the Fen Tigers, their blades flashing orange and black against the torchlight in the night.

I couldn't look. I turned tail and ran with the others, once again following that madman Van Buskirk deep into Wickern Fen.

VI: D.R.E.A.D.G.E.

We made our way quickly through the marsh. Visibility was low -- it was raining, the hour was late, and Van Buskirk carried no torch to better stay hidden. We weren't wearing our waders, so we were soaked, but it hardly mattered to us -- we knew who was on our tail.

The mad Dutchman took us on a slightly longer meandering path to the barn, to Dreadge, to lose the Fen Tigers. He shook them off, but they knew exactly where we were headed anyway.

As we approached Dreadge, the sky was lit a queer colour. The stars shone brighter than normal... sounds daft, but they did. The Fen was lit up as though by moonlight, but there was no moon in the sky. I did a double-take then -- hold on, the sky!

I hadn't seen it since arriving in that cursed Fen. But there it was, the night sky, in all its glory, glowing unhealthily greenish through a large clear patch in the clouds above the barn.

It was foggy all around the barn area, so a lot was still obscured at ground-level, but it had dispersed in the atmosphere above. Odd, I thought, that the stars would only be visible here. I had to look away, because I felt that they were calling to me and it made me queasy.

I heard a low thrumming noise, obviously the machine, reverberating against the barn walls. Above that, I could hear a higher-pitched rhythmic lilting. It was unwholesome. It made my ears itch.

Chanting, I thought with a shudder.

I can't tell you what they were chanting, but it wasn't Dutch, I know that much. This sounded completely alien, like human tongues shouldn't be pronouncing the syllables. And I swear, the way the sounds slipped and slithered into your ears... human ears definitely weren't supposed to be hearing them.

My teeth were on edge, my skin crawled, and my inner ears itched with the effort of listening. This was the same language as the one Van Buskirk's big book was written in, I thought. That's what it sounded like when chanted aloud... I couldn't hope to replicate it myself.

I saw, as we came closer to the barn, that it was emitting a foul green glow. The sullen Dutchmen - a great deal more of them than last time, I have no idea where they'd been hiding - were standing around the barn in a big circle, eyes raised towards the sky.

They stood and chanted their mournful song to the stars... it was hypnotic. It was horrible. Since last time I was here, they'd ditched the bulky coats they were wearing to reveal black robes beneath. The same as Van Buskirk's.

I remember thinking, then, that I'd gone too far. You might laugh -- obviously, I'd been in too deep for days at this point. But that was when I knew: I'd gotten myself mixed up in something that not only wasn't worth the pay, any amount of pay, but which was truly unholy.

I was witnessing the kind of rite that only the maddest preachers would have ever warned about. The kind of scare-story you'd dismiss as being too silly. But no, take it from me -- folk like this really do exist, and they might well be in some godforsaken corner of the world right now, all dressed up, singing their infernal hymns to the sky.

I saw that fences had been erected since our last visit. This is what Van Buskirk must have gone to oversee... they were erected in a circle around us; we had slipped through a gap. Behind us, an ominous figure in those ubiquitous black robes pushed another fence panel over the gap and began to hammer it into the ground.

We were enclosed.

Whatever Van Buskirk was trying to uncover was right here, in this little pool area just in front of the barn. The water in the rest of the bog seemed to be of little concern. The pool was draining alarmingly quickly; obviously there was no way to stop the rest of the bog-water filling in the hole, but Dreadge drained it faster than the Fen could replace it.

I'd only arrived a few minutes ago, and even then I could see a marked difference in the water level. In fact, I was even walking a bit freer and easier, because so much had drained from around our feet.

"Alright, Van Buskirk. You got us here. What's the plan?" I asked.

"Plan? Everything is going to plan already. My men are busy

operating the machine," he replied.

"Operating the machine, is that what you call it!" Coggins shouted, "I've never seen an engineer doing that!" He gestured toward the ring of chanting figures.

"As I may have intimated already," Van Buskirk drawled, "there is a lot that the likes of you don't understand about my machine."

Van Buskirk really pissed me off with that remark. Five of us had died for this. I lost my temper.

"Listen, you skinny specky bastard," I said, spittle flying, sticking my finger into his chest.

He batted my hand away with superlative strength and speed, belying his emaciated frame. He was swamped in his robes, with his hood up, so I could only see the smallest hint of his gaunt features in the green starlight. He drew himself up to his full height, which was very tall indeed.

I was dumbstruck. I have, quite honestly, started small-scale gang warfare over less disrespect than I'd just been shown. But this was the first time I'd ever been successfully intimidated by one man. I didn't know what that man really was, never mind who he really was.

When he saw that I wouldn't reply, he turned and sloshed through the bog to the barn. He said over his shoulder, "Five minutes. Possibly even less… the astrolabe is only accurate to within one minute. And then, you can leave this world behind!" He threw his arms wide, and waded off toward the barn.

I grumbled under my breath. The lads looked sidelong at me, shocked and probably disgusted that I'd kept so quiet.

The money, I remember thinking, the money. None of this was worth it, but I sure as hell didn't want to leave with nothing.

Suddenly, we heard a roaring from the other side of the fence. From our poor vantage point, it could have been an army. There were a few of the robed men holding the fences, with weapons drawn, but nowhere near enough of them.

We stood there nervously, five men, half the strength of our unit depleted. Instinctively, we formed our back-to-back circle, although it was a lot smaller and tighter than usual. Honestly, if I wasn't closed-in by fences, I might well have just ran away.

I don't know how long we stood there for, a couple of minutes perhaps, with the roaring growing louder.

The fences started to shake and buckle. We saw flames lick the top of some of the panels. It wasn't raining above our little patch of cloudless sky, so the flames leapt up eagerly and spread to nearby panels.

The first fence came down, only about thirty seconds after the fires had begun. At the same time, I saw dark figures clambering over the top of other fences, even ones that were on fire, such was their desperation. They cared not for blisters or callouses. They erupted over those fences like a forceful inferno.

The robed Dutchmen did their best to put up a fight but didn't manage to delay the Fen Tigers for even a minute. I even saw the scarecrow-outline of what could only be our mad landlady from The Stars Align inn; they'd obviously rallied everybody they had at their disposal to try to stop Van Buskirk.

I thought about that man then, and I seethed with anger.

I thought about Jock's ankles snapping and his screams as he went down beneath fifteen fiery blades. I thought about Riggs and Rugely, lying dead in their beds, probably still burning in the inn. Blakey and his mate would still have been bobbing about in the very parts of the bog they'd died in.

I know the Fen Tigers were the culprits, but they weren't exactly to blame, were they? The blame lay solely at the doorstep of Van Buskirk, for leading us here in the first place, and for riling up the locals with his unwholesome deeds.

I shook my head with gritted teeth. I was here to defend Van Buskirk, I thought. For a lot of money. I braced myself for the oncoming flurry of furious Fenmen.

The storm of steel, the clash of blades, the brawl in the bog… never actually materialised.

I blinked, stunned, still stood there in a fighting stance. My legs were like tingling lead, but I realised I was bracing them against nothing. The Fen Tigers and the regular villagers of Wickern were running straight past us.

I looked into their eyes on the way past, and saw not fury, but fear. These men were scared witless, and yet they were running toward the source of the danger in a mad last-ditch attempt to stop it all from happening.

They ran toward the barn, screaming, throwing their weapons, launching rocks from slings, with all the fierce bravery of cornered tigers.

That was when me and the lads had a change of heart.

"Fuck this," I shouted above the din. Seeing the looks on their faces, I knew I had more in common with the local Fenmen than with foreign occultist freaks like Van Buskirk. They were just honest English blokes trying to look after their own interests, but unlike me, these lot might well have been trying to save the world, too.

"You all thinking what I'm thinking?" Coggins shouted.

One of the other lads broke the circle and said, "stop him?"

"Aye! We owe that bastard nothing!" I roared.

With the memory of our fallen friends spurring us on, we charged toward the barn, screaming.

I remember finding it much easier to run. I looked down. I was barely making a splash. How long had it been? Surely not five minutes? I looked toward the centre of the pool that Dreadge had been draining. The water level was shockingly low... a pit had been unveiled, with fairly steep sides.

Stinking marsh gases rose from the mud, and some even flashed their ethereal green flames. I thought then about Everett, the cart-driver, and his fear of the "lantern-men", the will o' the wisps the Fen was famous for. If only those Lantern-men were the worst thing I had to fear tonight, I thought.

We charged on toward the barn, hoping to get to it in time before Dreadge completed its function, but I swear, it was though time was stretching and squeezing. Our feet weren't covering as much distance. The barn was close one moment and miles away the next. My gut lurched back and forth, like I was on a boat on a stormy sea.

Just as the first wave of Fen Tigers fell upon the ring of chanting "engineers", we heard a deep thunk sound that reverberated through our entire bodies. It felt more like an instantaneous earthquake underfoot.

The water between my toes swept away; as through some sort of plug had been pulled. The water was running from Wickern Fen quicker than the bathwater from a draining tub. But running to where?

Had the banks of the Ouse been breached, I thought? Was the Fen running into the river?

No.

I saw that every single one of the villagers had stopped in their tracks. They stared toward the middle of the pit. With creeping dread, I turned my head to look.

Unearthed at the bottom of the pit was a monolith. Its surface shifted and swirled before my very eyes, as though it couldn't decide what form it wanted to take.

There was a plinth at the bottom, stuck in the undulating slime at the bottom of the bog, a shape which should have been square. It poked out at odd angles that I didn't think squares were capable of.

I understood from seeing the plinth that it was some sort of statue. A statue of what, you ask? I couldn't possibly say. It gives me a headache to think about it. It wriggled and writhed as though it was covered with eels.

Who erected this statue? Were they human, proto-human? Something else entirely?

I have no idea, and even now, I still don't want to know. The curiosity which led me here had uncovered such secrets as to almost drive me mad already; I wasn't about to go digging further, and I never will.

All was silent. Even the chanting had stopped. The locals stood there in slack-jawed anguish, staring at the statue.

I looked toward the barn. Van Buskirk came out, looking like the Devil himself in his sweeping black robes, arms held out toward the statue. He walked toward it. His face was hidden beneath the hood, but I know that that freak would have been grinning from ear-to-ear.

Above us, light blazed suddenly. I looked up. The stars above, the very same stars which illuminated us with their pale green light, were aligning. Don't ask me how I knew, but I knew. I'd read the strange characters in Van Buskirk's book.

When I looked at the stars then, and even when I look at them now, it's just like reading the characters on the front of that old tome. I knew the stars were perfectly aligned because… well.

You wouldn't understand.

At this moment, the Fen Tigers and the locals screamed and shouted. They all ran away toward the fences and the Fen beyond. It was chaos, utter mayhem.

In the sickly starlight, I could see that some of them even fell upon each other, wild-eyed, scratching and slashing and stabbing and skewering and… what on Earth, I thought? Had they gone mad?

I felt alright. I mean, if I looked at that statue for any longer, I might have went even madder than I already am, but I wasn't about to start tearing my comrades' eyes out or anything…

I looked at Coggins, who was busily biting the throat out of one of the other lads.

"Fucking hell!" I remember shouting, the last words I'd utter in Wickern Fen, and a rather accurate description of the entire place and my experiences there.

I didn't even bother looking for the other two lads, and broke off running back toward the direction we'd come. The village of Wickern, believe it or not, was the closest thing to safety I could think of. At least there was a good solid road out of the place.

I took one last look over my shoulder, and saw that the robed Dutchmen were all completely fine. They walked slowly toward the statue with their arms held out in reverence. Dreadge was abandoned in its big, ugly barn. Its purpose had been served.

The horizon seemed impossibly close. I saw the mad landlady of The Stars Align with her hedgerow hair disappear over it, chasing one of her patrons with a meat cleaver, only to reappear on the opposite horizon behind me, still running in the same direction, still chasing her quarry.

She fell on him with sickening glee.

I felt sick, not with horror at that savagery, but with trying to wrap my head around the geographical shenanigans I'd just witnessed. Still, though, I didn't feel like I had to submerge myself into that awful orgy of violence.

I wondered: why was it only me and those Dutch freaks who weren't affected? I wasn't in immediate danger, so I stopped to look. I could make out Van Buskirk's lanky frame very easily, approaching the end of the pit.

Like a lightning bolt, I realised: the book. The characters in the book. Not one other member of my group had read those characters. I assume that none of the locals had either, not even the ones who ransacked the garret, as that arcane tome was under Van Buskirk's notebooks.

My vague knowledge of that strange star-language saved me, while my friends tore each other apart in wet, dirty mud. With my last ounce of bravery, I ran toward Van Buskirk. He wasn't getting away with this, I thought.

The money didn't matter any more, and neither did his bullshit swamp rituals, but he'd used me and my friends like pawns on a chessboard. He knew that we'd end up murdering each other in that Fen as soon as his prize was uncovered.

I aimed my knife as surely as I could. I've hit targets from further away - just watch me play darts, I'm a demon. He was as good as dead, I was sure of it: I launched the knife.

Van Buskirk turned to look at me. He simply stood there, bathed in green light, at the rim of the pit. He threw back his hood and I could see his eyes, fixed on me, and a fiendish grimace splitting his face.

The knife, in mid-air... I know you won't believe me, but you've believed me thus far, right? Right?

The knife's trajectory swerved to the left to avoid Van Buskirk. No, there was no wind, no nothing, I won't hear of it: the knife swerved toward the pit as though magnetised to that horrible monolith.

Whether it really was just a strange material property of that monstrosity unearthed from the bog, or whether the thing was consciously protecting him, I will never know.

Anyway, I know when I'm beaten. I turned tail and ran all the way to Wickern.

Epilogue

So, that's where my tale ends.

How did I escape, you ask? Well, it's a bit of a blur...

I remember the Fen becoming dryer and dryer as the night went on. It was pissing down with rain, but the ground drank it down faster than it could fall from the heavens.

How big was the space uncovered beneath the bog, I thought? What ancient spaces were being flooded by the waters of the Earth, now that the plug had been pulled?

What would stir from beneath?

I heard something which could have been the roar of some terrible beast, or just a thunderclap. I ran all the quicker.

I made it back to the village a couple of hours after dawn. It shouldn't have taken that long, but things are all wrong now. Distances don't work properly, haven't you noticed?

The world's unravelling, coming apart like the threads of an old blanket. Call me mad all you want, I know you've noticed it too...

Anyway, Wickern was abandoned when I got there. The inn was little more than a smoldering shell. I saw a cart in the middle of the street, tipped over on its side.

I saw Everett, the cart-driver, impaled against a wall with the very hay fork that he would have used in the stable. Poor Everett, and whoever had killed him, had not escaped the madness that befell the marsh.

As I've said, he was a miserable bastard, but he was a good bloke nonetheless. Much like ourselves, he probably got involved for the pay, and didn't get out quick enough.

I heard whinnying and found Sugarlumps just around the corner, obviously distressed at the death of her master. I figured that now was as good a time as any to get over my fear of horses, and leapt up on her back, and rode her all the way to Cambridge at double-time.

You've seen the newspaper clipping I brought, yes? From the Cambridge Observer? 'Remote Inn Burned Down in Mysterious Fire, Villagers Nowhere to be Found', reads the headline.

As for that profane machine, D.R.E.A.D.G.E. - the Grave Ex-humer part makes a bit more sense to me now. I don't know what that statue was, or who could have "buried" it underneath the Fen, but I suspect they did it for a reason, and those Fen Tigers were proud protectors of its "grave."

Generations of them… but it only takes one nutcase to com-pletely undo everything. One nutcase, and a few greedy hench-men to back him up.

And now, that really is the end of my story. So how about you buy me another pint? I've kept you all well entertained, haven't I?

What am I doing back here in London?

Well, I spent those five pounds that Van Buskirk gave me on cheap tickets to America, trying to escape what's coming. But I've seen the reports from over there, too. The swamps are draining. The Great Lakes are declining rapidly.

Exactly the same as over here, isn't it? Surely you've heard about Loch Ness? It's lost a fifth of its water in a month! And the Lake District? Folk are calling it the Pond District! Where's it all going?

You don't want to know. You'll go mad if you try to find out.

All I know is, you'll want to keep safe, and stay hidden… or you'll end up like my pals, ripping each other apart for no good reason.

Me? I'll be alright. I know their language, remember? Although I'm not sure I want to survive to see what the world will look like, when the inky tombs beneath us are opened to the skies above.

Lord knows what will be unearthed when our waters disperse and the stars align.

Prestwick's Project

The wine doesn't taste so sweet when I think about the cost. Neither does the brandy. The travelling, the hotels, the sights, the sounds... I can't truly enjoy any of it. I'm just running away. Nothing seems so swish when I sit and truly consider the cost.

Oh, I'm not talking about the money. I've got plenty of that thanks to Professor Prestwick. Thanks to my involvement in his little project, there'll be a lot more of... them, and a lot less of us. It'll have started in the big cities, the University towns - seems like anywhere with a lab with powerful enough equipment was collaborating in that project over the Summer.

The cities aren't safe - that's why I took the money and ran. What choice did I have? I got as far away as possible. And when that wasn't far enough, I kept going. I'm a nomad now - but I can't quite escape. I'm always running away, but certain things seem to follow me. The sky is too black. I fear that I'm no longer in tune with the "real world" that I used to inhabit.

I almost got into trouble trying to buy weapons. Guns - but guns won't be of any use. Guns, famously, obey the laws of physics. They do not. What was I thinking?

I was thinking, I suppose, about my own safety - but what can I do, other than prolong the inevitable? Are they even after me, or are they happy to let me go on, continuing Prestwick's project?

Despite me drinking and cavorting as much as Prestwick's money allows, I can't forget some of the things I saw back at the Lab during that project; they come to me in the night; they leave me screaming and twisting and turning. And the consequences are impossible to ignore, as is the fact that I had my own part to play in bringing them about.

I was drafted onto Prestwick's project a few months ago... or has it only been weeks? A year, even? The timescales are hazy, for reasons that will become clear. The project started fairly innocuously. I'd been brought onto these "Summer Projects" before, due to my good grades and extensive extracurricular activities. I was happy to take this one, much like I was with the others - they provided solid money over the Summer months between University terms, and sometimes they involved very little work.

We'd be paid to tinker with cool, expensive machines, take a bit of data here and there, plug some numbers into a computer... and we'd have plenty of banter all the while. Afterwards, we'd be off to the pub - ideal.

Sure, the bigwig professor we were doing the research for would take all the glory, but that's the way of things, isn't it? We all yearned for that. We all aspired to be that professor one day, and extracurricular activities (and being taken advantage of) were a given for anybody that wanted to achieve such lofty heights.

When my housemate Mark and I were contacted by Professor Fucking Prestwick, of all people, we were over the moon. The man was a legend, the most famous scientist at our University by a long way. He'd been on the tele! We thought that getting our names on a paper with him would have been a golden ticket for our careers.

We hadn't seen him for weeks before the end of last term; we thought he was ill, but rumours abounded that he'd been playing with a new machine. Some new-fangled thing to measure and model certain frequencies… I didn't understand it at the time, and I'm still not sure I understand the intricacies of it now. Either way, it was little more than a cover story.

I now know what that thing does, and it has little to do with mere measurement. Professor Prestwick had been in contact with some shady characters, and he'd been pursuing some avenues of research that were thoroughly unwholesome. You can't be shocked that a man of such searching intellect would go rogue, I suppose, should he spot some irregularities in his experiments. But go rogue he did… to the detriment of much more than his sanity.

We knew nothing of this at the time, though. Mark and I were simply offered the chance to collaborate with him on a new project over email. Curiously, we'd been asked not to tell anybody else. We'd told each other, obviously. We shared a house. We shouted and punched the air in unison upon reading our own individual emails, so it would've been a hard thing for us to hide from each other.

Maybe this was some top-secret thing that he didn't want just any pleb student knowing about, we said over a pint that evening; maybe only the most competent students would have been invited. Maybe he didn't want the others getting jealous. Or, screw it, maybe we just won a raffle! Whatever the reason, we weren't turning him down.

The next morning, we walked through the web of corridors in the Physics department, up and down many staircases, and across a myriad of confusing bridges between the angular Brutalist buildings that made up this end of the University.

One corridor was closed for refurbishment, so we had to take a detour through one of the undergraduate Physics laboratories. It was a bit eerie being in the lab whilst it was empty, no students, only neatly-packed boxes of equipment and pristine work surfaces. Some notebooks and pens had been carelessly left on a few of the benches, and we didn't care to glance at the feverish scribbles contained therein. Our footsteps echoed through the lab and then back into the maze of corridors.

We finally reached Prestwick's office, an expertly hidden room occupied by a man who often wished to be left alone to his research. 9 A.M. sharp, as requested, wearing our lab coats, trailed by a whiff of coffee and cheap deodorant. Nervously, I knocked at the door where PROF. PRESTWICK was emblazoned upon a metal plaque fixed to the wood.

"Enter," I heard him shout, muffled through the door. We walked in, and I couldn't stop my face from twisting - the smell in there hit me like a brick to the face.

It was a smell I'd become greatly familiar with over the coming weeks. Acrid. A sharp, sulphurous, eggy smell... oddly chemical but hard to place. It smelled like a hundred things at once, all of them unpleasant. Not disgusting, like sewage, but... yes, unpleasant, strange, and incredibly distracting.

I looked for the man in amongst the piles of books and opened boxes. There were opened books on every surface, books resting on boxes, books stacked upon other books, books resting on the opened drawers in the desk... as though he had been hunting for some specific thing to aid his research. The more I looked around, though, the more it seemed like he'd been scrabbling for every piece of knowledge he could get his hands on, all at once... the subjects of the books were so disparate.

The man himself, Professor Prestwick, was little more than a pale shadow in the corner of his office. He was standing on a chair, reaching for something on his top shelf, and he looked thin. Really thin. We were shocked. Maybe he had been ill after all, we remarked afterwards.

He reached what he desired, grabbed it and brought it down: another book. I peered at the spine: Computational Methodologies, volume 6. Interesting, I thought, not the kind of thing that Prestwick was known for, but the man was obviously branching out, given the state of his room.

"Please, gentlemen, have a seat," said Prestwick, in a raspier voice than normal. The bloke sounded rough. His tongue sounded like it was too big for his mouth, as though it were swollen,

as though he was uncomfortable using it. His speech was oddly modulated, not at all like the commanding voice he used to
address lecture theatres of hundreds of rapturous students; but,
I supposed, he was unlikely to use his "lecturer voice" here in his
cramped little office, wasn't he?

We looked around awkwardly. Despite his request, there was
nowhere to sit. There were two boxes in the middle of the floor,
with stacks of books open on them. He gestured towards them.

With confused looks on our faces, Mark and I asked him if he
wanted the books moved.

"What, why?" he snapped.

"In case we ruin them?" Mark said.

"Oh. I see. But there are more books underneath them," he
answered.

I shook my head and sat down upon the open book in front of
me. Mark did likewise. It was the Physics department - we were
used to social awkwardness. This was strange behaviour though,
even for Physics, and especially for Prestwick. The man was
normally very charismatic, having led numerous lectures and
having starred in the television show, but I looked at him then
with some concern.

The man's normally jolly, chubby face had become sunken,
almost like he'd been on drugs or something, but I knew he
wouldn't have been daft enough to get into anything like that at
his age. Still, though, his eyes had retreated into dark hollows.

He was pale and gaunt, to the point that his old clothes no
longer fit him properly, so that his tweed jacket hung loose
and his trousers sagged sadly. The man was a mess - he hadn't
had a haircut in too long, and wiry facial hair hid his normally
clean-shaven visage.

The eyes, though, they stick with me most of all… he always
had somewhat of a piercing, searching expression, somehow
intelligent-looking eyes. But now they looked hungry and black.
He wasn't merely searching for knowledge, he was ravenous, he
wanted to know more. He had the look of a man obsessed.

I looked around at the opened books around me. Books about world history, geography, culture, computers, science...

I looked back at Professor Prestwick. There was a heavy silence in the room. I spoke up: "We're here about the-"

"Project?" Prestwick butted in.

"Y-," I began, caught off guard, "well, yes."

Professor Prestwick nodded furiously, looking between Mark and me. "Keep it quiet, gentlemen," he said, "only four other students have been asked. The other members of the faculty don't even know. Can you two keep a secret?"

"Yes, Professor," I began nervously, "but why does this have to be a secret? Will we get in trouble if anyone finds out we're working with you? I don't want to risk my degree."

"Don't worry about any of that. I can authorise this. But I have been warned against tinkering with my new machine... the faculty said it was bad for my health, you see."

He looked at us, wild-eyed, dishevelled, clammy. The acrid smell in the room seemed to emanate from him, now that I'd had time to acclimatise to the room. Mark and I looked sidelong at each other but said nothing. We didn't want to disagree with him, even though he was so visibly unhealthy and behaved so erratically.

He went on, "if you're interested, and I know you are, we're going to get to grips with that machine... I was making headway before they stopped me. The rewards will be well worth it. Upon seeing the payslip, you will understand why I didn't advertise this job publicly. Are you, then? Interested?"

So, to my regret, due to a mixture of curiosity, greed, and fear, we went along with it. We wanted our name on whatever he was publishing. We wanted illustrious careers like him, we wanted tenured positions, we wanted money, we wanted fame.

I couldn't wait to get out of his office, but just to try to break the strange tension and build some rapport, I thought I'd make a comment on the way out.

"Computational Methods, eh? I haven't read much on that since First Year. Will the project deal much with that kind of thing?"

I turned around, from where I'd opened the door, to find him sat in complete stillness, where he'd been chatting to us. As if somebody had pressed the pause button.

His eyes darted to mine.

"I hope so, I hope so," he muttered under his breath. He said, louder, "there might not be a computer powerful enough. Where might I find a very powerful computer?"

"Uh…" I looked at Mark, nonplussed.

"CERN? In Switzerland?" he said, equally confused.

The Professor began to scribble on a notepad. "How am I spelling that?" he asked.

"Professor Prestwick," Mark said, "it's the huge nuclear research facility up in Switzerland. You've delivered lectures on it… I've been to a couple of them. They must have some serious computational power there."

"Switzerland, you say," the Professor went on, scribbling. He flashed us that hungry, searching look, and said under his breath, "computational power…" before returning to his notes. He even wrote strangely, gripping the pen with four fingertips and his thumb clamped onto the opposite side, and he moved his wrist wildly to produce scribbles on his notepad. He didn't look at the notepad while he was doing it - he just stared straight ahead.

With this, I shook my head subtly at Mark and frowned, giving him a signal with my thumb - let's get out of here. Just as we were about to do so, I caught sight of his coat stand, which had a crumpled leather coat hanging from it. I did a double-take - in my peripheral vision, it was like there was a person standing there in the corner of the room, but when I looked, it was definitely just a coat.

I put it down to simply being nervous; I was jumpy. This meeting had been so strange and uncomfortable that I was scared of my own shadow - the Professor's behaviour had unsettled me deeply.

It was all Mark and I could talk about on the way home. We were excited but also spooked. The promised cash - we didn't know the amount, but we were skint students. To think I'd been considering working in a bar over the Summer! By the sounds of this, I'd be able to start saving towards a house deposit or a car or something.

But the toll this project had already taken on the Professor was shocking. We convinced ourselves that he was just ill - he had the flu or something, I said, and Mark nodded along, looking pensive. There was no reason why somebody couldn't be both flu-ridden and consumed by their research at the same time, I supposed.

I was kidding myself, though. Deep down, I knew something was up. But it was just one of those things - you know it's wrong, but greed, or lust, or pride, or some other sin leads you down the wrong path anyway. You don't want to believe that it's wrong, so you choose not to.

We got little sleep that night, and I felt awful in the morning. I'd tossed and turned all night. Through the paper-thin walls of our shit student house, I'd heard Mark doing the same on his creaky old bed. I didn't have nightmares or anything, I just felt a deep-seated uneasiness, and my mind had raced with possibilities and wonder. I couldn't drift off to sleep with all this going on.

I swore that that smell had followed me home, I kept catching the faintest whiff of it, just on the edge of smelling, but when I sniffed more to investigate further, it was gone... just the usual smell of sweaty socks that permeated my room. I asked Mark about it in the morning. Same thing with him.

We showed up at the time we'd been given in the email: 6 P.M. in the basement laboratory. We were no stranger to late nights in the lab, but this was a very late start. The security guard, a new one I'd never seen before, checked our IDs and nodded us through. There are millions of pounds worth of equipment down there, lasers and supercomputers and the like, so it's guarded at all times by a cohort of very bored security staff.

I wondered whether Professor Prestwick had told them to let us through specifically, or if this man was just checking that we were students at the University. I was second-guessing everything after my encounter with Prestwick. I dreaded seeing him again, but I was also morbidly curious about his machine and his project.

We turned a corner in the basement and found him there in the low light, surrounded by the other four students on the project.

Much to my surprise, he was in better spirits than when we'd seen him just one day beforehand. He stood tall and proud, still a little pale in the face, but he'd had a wash at least, and a shave. He seemed less frantic than the day before, standing there quite cool and collected.

I was still concerned for the man's health. He had colour in his cheeks, but they were no less gaunt. He still wasn't wearing clothes that fit his newly-skinny frame, but ill-fitting clothes were not an uncommon sight in the Physics department.

We took our places beside the other students. I recognised them from lectures and labs but didn't know their names. One of them looked at me and raised his eyebrow quizzically, as if to voice the exact same concerns I had about the professor.

Prestwick looked down at us all now through round spectacles, with those same ravenous eyes, and smiled an unnerving un-smile… his mouth moved, but it wasn't joined by the necessary eye or cheek movements that make a smile genuine. I smiled in return, but, inwardly, my flesh crawled. It wouldn't be the last time I'd see that awful un-smile.

He ushered us toward the back of the room, towards what I thought was a fire-exit into the underground car park. He opened the door to reveal a tunnel - odd, I thought - and the confused expressions of my colleagues let me know that this was a surprise to all of us. None of us could afford to drive, and the parking here was strictly staff-only, so I suppose we didn't know the layout as well as we thought. Still, though, we all definitely expected a car park to be there.

We walked through this tunnel - very nondescript, concrete walls, concrete floor, no decoration - and through another door into a larger room that housed a huge, cuboid machine with a door in the middle of it. To the left of the room were a few com-puters - big things, very impressive-looking - and a couple of desks and chairs. There were screens attached to the computers, but there were no windows. We were still underground.

The central machine was jet-black. I had no idea what kind of metal it was made out of, or what it was painted with… it was vanta-black. I'd read about it - the pigment absorbed almost 100% of visible light in the spectrum, so it appeared like the absence of colour rather than the colour black. Seeing so much of it at once was hypnotic - like staring into the black void of space.

All of our eyes were drawn to it, and all of us stared, in silence - until Professor Prestwick clicked his fingers.

"Gentlemen," he began, "behold my machine. These things are very new, and quite a few major research facilities have been equipped with one." His eyes glittered. Must have been the light reflecting off his glasses, I thought.

Mark raised his hand timidly.

"Yes?"

"What's it called?"

"It doesn't have a name yet."

"Oh."

There was an awkward silence.

Another lad cleared his throat and said, "what does it do?"

"It… measures frequencies," said the Professor. This appeared to be enough. He turned around and walked to the computers at the side of the room.

We all looked at each other, shrugging.

One student, a small ginger lad, piped up and said "what kind of frequencies?"

"Well, I don't know yet," said the Professor, "that's what you're here to find out."

That same ginger lad put his hands on his hips and exhaled sharply. He said, annoyed, "can we have some more information please? And has this passed the necessary safety checks? Should we be working on this, as students?"

Professor Prestwick turned around, with that devilish gleam in his eyes, and simply said: "no."

"Right," said the ginger lad, "I'm not having this. I'm going home."

There were a couple of grumbles and two other lads followed him out of the room.

Prestwick looked at those of us who remained and smiled another un-smile. "Think you three can handle it?" he asked. "There might be extra in it for you."

I knew this was dodgy, and I voiced my unease, but more than our already-healthy pay was too much to pass up. And, I hate to admit it, but this vanta-black machine had drawn me into its mysterious aura. I wanted to know more - much like Prestwick, I was hungry to know more. This was secret stuff, and it was cool, and I'm sure Mark and the other remaining students felt the same. It felt like cutting-edge science, the kind we all dreamed about, with the added romanticism of it being somehow clandestine.

We were hooked.

Prestwick showed us to the terminals, showed us the parts of the machine, showed us some buttons and dials. He didn't give us many details. Apparently we were to be mere research monkeys, pulling levers and recording results. Why this couldn't be automated, I didn't know, but I wasn't about to suggest that and cheat myself out of good money and my name on a paper.

He opened the door, and I swear, it was like looking into space… A hollow, empty region of space, where the stars had long-ago winked out of existence. The whole inside of the machine was made of the same vanta-black material.

We walked through the door. It was a whole vanta-black room, big enough for us all to stand inside. On one wall was a round dial, white-backed, and although it was a dull-white, it stood out so starkly against its ultra-black surroundings that it could have been a lonely little star.

He walked to the dial and turned it with one hand, motioning for us to come look with the other. There were numbers, simply 1, 2, 3, etc., on the dial, which were visible in a little window within the dial's face. He showed us how to rotate the dial, clockwise, to expose the series of numbers, one after the other in the little window.

After hitting 9, the dial would go back to 1. A circular dial - seemed simple enough. I wish I'd investigated further, but at the time, that's what I remember thinking: seems simple enough.

We exited the vanta-room.

"The aim, gentlemen, is to twist the dial through various combinations of numbers, and press this button here," Prestwick gestured to a button set into one of the terminals, "and then record the output on the screens into notebooks. Is that clear?"

"Yes," I said. I couldn't resist picking at one of the many loose threads he'd left. "Why can't the computers just record it?"

"I'd rather there were no electronic records just yet, gentlemen," said the mysterious Professor. "Write with your pens in your notebooks, and then clear the results from the terminals."

"And then what?"

"Then do it again. Rotate the dial again, differently, more. Keep doing it."

"What are you expecting to happen?"

"I don't know," the Professor said, and flashed us one final un-smile for the evening. "That's what we're down here trying to find out!"

With this, he turned and went to exit the room.

"Wait," I said, "where are you going?"

"To Aldwich University, to help set up their machine," he answered. "This is somewhat of a collaborative project."

I had asked that question rhetorically - what I meant to say were things like 'why are you leaving so soon?', 'where are you going?', and 'I am very confused, please tell me more', but the Professor had turned around and closed the door before I had a chance to process his response.

"What the hell," I said matter-of-factly.

"This is trouble," said the other lad, who later introduced himself as Scott, "but I'm into it."

Mark laughed. "Me too."

"Prestwick's a weird one, isn't he?" I asked, still gobsmacked by his demeanour.

"He's not like this in lectures," Scott said, "I know that much. And on that science TV show a few years ago, he was the life of the party, wasn't he?"

"I know, yeah!" I said, happy that somebody else had noticed the apparent change in his behaviour, "it must have all been scripted or something."

"Maybe we'll be that weird after messing about with this thing for a few days," Mark said.

"Jeez, I hope not," I replied, and we set to work.

We were in there for what seemed like hours, rotating the dial, recording sequences of numbers in our books, and recording outputs from the computers. The computers simply gave answering strings of numbers - different every time, even when using the same set of numbers in the vanta-room.

This was boring work, but we were still fascinated by the machine and what it was actually doing. We took it in turns - one of us would be inside the machine, one of us reading out the computer terminal's answers, and the other writing them down in a notebook.

We deduced, from rhythmic hums and vibrations in the floor, that the real machinery in this thing was under the vanta-room itself. We could see cables reaching upward into the ceiling, too, disappearing up through a hole at the back of the wider room.

We decided, after some fruitless hours, to start expanding the strings of numbers we used. We'd stuck to 3 and 4-digit strings, but we started to do 8, 9, even fifteen-digit strings, just to see what happened. Mostly nothing, but whoever stood inside the machine did detect small shifts in the vibrations beneath them.

This was too subjective though, and the computer terminals simply gave answering strings - they petered out after 8 or 9 digits, so we stuck around there, discovering that 6 digits was the ideal length to produce both full answers and meaningful shifts in the machine's vibrations.

I became somewhat exasperated with this and decided we'd been at it long enough for the night. It was past midnight, and I wanted to go back to bed. I'd slept awfully, after all. Mark was eager to leave, too.

Scott, though, wanted to stay. He looked up with a bit of a gleam in his eyes. He'd had a full flask of coffee and was beginning to show signs of the same obsession I'd noticed in Professor Prestwick.

He said to me, "Are you joking? We're actually making progress here!"

"What are you on about, mate? We're rotating a fucking dial and listening for the hum. This is all completely meaningless," I said, flustered. "It's a joke! I'll do it for the pay, but until Prestwick gives us a bit more info, there's no such thing as 'progress' here."

"You're too thick to understand," Scott snapped. "Watch."

He got up and walked inside the vanta-room. We heard six clicks - six turns of the dial - six numbers entered. He came out, talking rapidly, half to us and half to himself, "The hum has been getting ever-so-slightly higher, but I could feel something in my chest, too, as though there were bass tones, pressure needing to be released, potential…"

Mark looked at me and shrugged.

Scott pressed the button set into the terminals, and there came a sudden loud twanging noise. I gasped, it being the loudest noise I'd heard all night; it started at an incredibly deep frequency, raising up as it oscillated back and forth, until it was an ear-splittingly high buzz. It left a ringing in my ears which took a few minutes to dissipate.

The terminals lit up - strings on strings of numbers came back, filling multiple pages.

"Hah! See!" Scott shouted, delighted. He ran back into the vanta-room, six more clicks, he came back out, he pressed the button again and eagerly looked at the screens.

Nothing.

He banged his fists on the keyboard and shouted, "NO!"

I shook my head, ears still ringing. "Look, mate, go home," I said, not unkindly. "Well done for recognising whatever pattern's at work here - that is progress - but we need to get some rest and get back at it tomorrow, alright?"

Scott said nothing, and frantically scratched away into his notebook with a cheap biro pen. I gave up.

Mark and I walked out of the room, out of the basement, and all the way back through the Physics department. I felt very strange, as though my eyes were more sensitive to light than before, but I blamed that on so much time spent in the vanta-room. My head buzzed, but that could have been the caffeine I'd been consuming to power through such a boring experiment, I thought.

It was very late.

We saw not a soul, not even security, which was odd. There'd normally be a few blokes lurking about in high-vis jackets, a few students burning the midnight oil, someone smoking a lonely cigarette on a bench.

The walk home, likewise, was bizarrely quiet. The noisy student parties that took place all Summer had apparently taken a reprieve for the night - not a peep from any of the houses. We saw nobody. The street lights were on, but it seemed oppressively dark - very strange, I thought, and I couldn't quite place what was bothering me about it... until I looked up.

The sky was jet-black. I know, I know, that's what colour it is at night, I know - but not like this. There were no stars, no clouds, no atmospheric gradation of blues and purples and blacks. I swear, the sky was vanta-black.

Sounds ridiculous, I know, and I didn't want to alarm Mark, so I didn't say anything. I wasn't convinced that it wasn't just paranoia, a mild visual effect produced by lack of sleep and having spent hours inside the vanta-room, so I studiously kept my head down, refusing to look at it. Only our footsteps echoed in the eerie silence, all the way home.

Now, that night I did have weird dreams - all about the

strange behaviour of those around me, and of being lost in a black void. I heard the noise again, but this time, it started high-pitched… I was hearing the oscillating twang, but this time in reverse. With a sense of dread, in my nightmare, I waited for it to get lower, lower, until with a BOOM it reached its climax. I sat bolt upright in bed, sweating.

I ran to the curtains and checked the sky - overcast, portions of baby blue visible through the gaps in the clouds. People out on the street below, walking, talking, laughing.

I breathed a sigh of relief and sank to my bedroom floor, shaking. The bizarre ride I'd been on had come to a stop, I thought, but then I remembered… our work with that infernal machine had only just begun.

We'd be back in that laboratory, when, this morning? This afternoon? Had Scott even left? He could still be in there, frantically spinning the dial and pushing the button.

I mulled this over as I pushed my breakfast around the plate moodily, not hungry enough for it. Mark, likewise, hadn't even made himself anything to eat. He stood there chugging black coffee. We looked like shit warmed up; maybe we'd begun our degeneration into the Professor's crazed state.

Were we really going to end up as weird as him? Was there something else going on here, something deeper? Why did it all feel so wrong? I dispelled the notion from my head - we were physicists. There could be nothing supernatural at work, we convinced ourselves hastily, laughing and joking as we got ready to leave. After sliding my breakfast off the plate and into the bin, I poured myself a coffee to go, and we left the house.

On the way out, I realised something that we'd missed on the way in: a ton of letters had been delivered. Weird. Normally we'd just get a few takeaway menus, a few bills maybe, but never this many in one day. Very strange, I thought, as the pile of letters crumpled behind the weight of the opening door, and we stepped outside.

I wish I'd bothered to check the dates on them.

On our way to the lab that morning, we passed the ginger lad who had piped up the previous evening, the one who'd walked away from Prestwick. He had grown an impressive amount of facial hair for one night, I thought… or did he have that beard last night? I couldn't quite remember. The lighting was poor down in the basement, after all.

He did a double-take as he saw us, as though recognising a pair of old acquaintances.

"H-Hey," he stuttered.

"Hello," I answered jovially, "think you made the right choice about Prestwick's Project, mate. It's absolutely nuts."

The ginger lad's demeanour changed. He looked around him, as though paranoid, as though he feared being watched or eavesdropped upon.

"Have you been…?" he said, urgently.

"Have we been what?" asked Mark abruptly. Mark had little time for nervous folk like this, people who beat around the bush, but I was more sympathetic.

"Calm down, lad," I said, "what's the matter?"

"We've… noticed some things. In the Physics department. Things aren't right."

"How do you mean?"

"I've been in the labs, I've been talking to folk - none of the instruments are working properly. Nothing's measuring the right values. I mean, they do sometimes, but other times, it's all wrong-"

"Calibration issues, then," Mark butted in, bemused. "Get one of the bigwigs or the lab techs to sort it out."

"No," he hissed, "that's what I'm saying, they aren't right, either - they laugh it off, they get confused, they forget things, they cover up mistakes, they're not the same, nobody's the same… they're all getting a bit like Prestwick! And I thought you two had disappeared, and Scott…" He trailed off.

I looked at him, concerned. He was wide-eyed, dishevelled.

Mark placed a hand on his shoulder and said, "mate. You're

getting a bit like Prestwick. Go and get some rest."

"Hang on," I said, "did you see Scott, then? Did he pull an all-nighter?"

At this, the already-pale ginger lad turned an even milkier shade. "I… I thought I saw him. In the labs. When I looked again, he wasn't there."

"Oh? Was it just somebody that looked like him?"

"…no."

Mark interjected again, "alright, then! See ya later!" He grabbed my arm and led me away. I turned back to look at the poor lad's grave visage; he looked back at me. I shuddered.

Further down the corridor, Mark said under his breath, "Fucking freak, man, what was he on? Just as well he isn't on the project."

"Mark, mate," I said, "I don't think I want to be on this project, either."

"What, like him? A ginger halfwit who can't calibrate equipment, who's too awkward to ask the staff for help? It's a nightmare working with that kind of person, I've had enough of them pulling my grades down in group projects. I'm not letting slackers like him cost me money as well."

With a heavy heart, I walked at Mark's side, cowed into silence by his thunderous mood. Mark did brighten up a bit when we were closer to the basement. He seemed to be quite excited about getting stuck back into Prestwick's research, and as we approached the staircase downward, we ran into the man himself coming out through the double-doors.

Professor Prestwick stood there, lean, proud, hands on his hips, apparently having sorted out his appearance since we met just the previous evening. He wore a well-fitted suit, with all the necessary accessories: pocket-square, tie, cufflinks. He looked back to his old self, but even better somehow. Slimmer, more refined, more sleek. Gone was the image of the merry, portly lecturer - he looked now like a catalogue model for poncey tweed suits.

"Ah, gentlemen!" he exclaimed, throwing his arms wide, "good to see you!"

His brightness took me off-guard. I had gotten too used to his strange, unhealthy demeanour.

"Back to continue the research! Your friend has made some good progress."

"Scott? Did he stay all night?" I asked.

"All night?" Prestwick was taken aback for a moment, but he blinked and in a flash he was back in charge of the conversation, "All night, of course! He may still be down there now, I'm not sure. I've been working on other things; I've not checked up on the machine in some time."

"Weren't you going to Aldwich University?" Mark asked, awe in his voice, "it's miles away. Have you gotten much sleep?"

"Sleep? No. There is no need for sleep when such important work is being done. Our colleagues in Aldwich report much the same successes as us; we edge ever closer to our goal."

"Professor," I began uneasily, "what is our goal?"

At this question, to my horror, Prestwick smiled the same un-smile that he'd done last time I saw him. A creepy, uncanny un-smile that was not joined by any of his other facial muscles. This betrayed to me that he was not alright; he was just as strange as he'd been, except now, he simply wore the right clothes... he looked the part, but he wasn't home. He was not himself. It just wasn't the same Prestwick that had delivered those scintillating lectures; it wasn't the bloke that was on that wildly popular science show.

The hairs on my arms stood on end, there was a sinking feeling in my gut, and I couldn't hide the look of disgust on my face.

"Don't worry about it," Prestwick said, "all will become clear in time. It is important that you don't know, as knowledge of the aim may colour your ability to take accurate data. With the random nature of tuning these frequencies, I cannot allow any biases in the recording. Better you keep going as you have been; your colleague Scott has made significant progress in the time you have been away."

"He didn't go to sleep, then?" Mark asked. I was still silent.

"I told you already. There is no need for sleep."

Mark and I looked at each other. Doubts flickered over Mark's face, but he shook them off quickly enough, and went on talking.

"Where are you going, then?"

"I'm jetting off to Switzerland," said the Professor emphatically, "my flight leaves in a few hours. Gentlemen, I must be going."

At this, he pushed past us and went on his way. I watched him go, and before he turned the corner, he looked back at me and flashed me one last un-smile, while his eyes and eyebrows stayed unnervingly put.

Mark rushed down the stairs to the basement, and I followed as fast as I could. I wanted to stop him, to ask him if he'd noticed that something was still off with Prestwick, but Mark was off; he was on a mission… he wanted that extra credit. Knowing Mark, he'd have been jealous that Scott received praise for making progress in his absence.

I followed him through the basement rooms and through the little fire escape door into the concrete tunnel that led to the room that housed Prestwick's vanta-black machine.

Scott, to my relief, was not there when we entered. Just to make sure, I opened the door to the vanta-room within the machine: nope, not in there either.

Seeing that my doubts about this project would not be entertained, I decided to get my head down and get to work. There was little else to do at that moment, and, after all, I was getting paid.

Mark and I discussed what to do next for the project, what data to take… this felt exhausting already. It needed automation. The words of the mad ginger kid played heavily on my mind; things were obviously stranger than they seemed.

Were we burying our heads in the sand here?

Were we to just keep mashing combinations of six figures into the dial and letting it rip, hoping for another horrible, ear-destroying noise? If anything, I wanted that never to happen again, but I supposed that wouldn't be aligned with Prestwick's aims.

I decided to check the notebook that Scott had left, wondering where he'd got to… now this freaked me out. I called Mark over. The notebook was almost full, as though Scott had been at this for weeks already. There were a couple of spent pens lying scattered over the desk, emptied of ink.

Mark picked up the book and started leafing through it.

I looked at him and said, "all that in one night?"

"Looks like it," came his reply, "but look at this."

He flipped open the notebook and went back a few pages from the most recent one, and pointed at an area of the page. I squinted and did a double-take. Upon the pages were sequences of… symbols, things that weren't numbers, in amongst the normal numbers.

I frowned and looked closer. I can't really describe the symbols - they were like runes, strange squiggles, but they were repeated, as though Scott had learned these new characters and was drawing them in place of numbers.

I saw, with some alarm, that he appeared to have filled the computer-response column with the same symbols. I looked at the computer - it had been wiped, as per Prestwick's request. We'd have to do some experiments if we wished to confirm whether the computer gave those symbols out… or whether Scott's brain had simply melted.

At the time, I believed it was the latter.

Mark and I walked into the vanta-room and went to the dial. We could see 7,8,9… hesitantly, I continued turning the dial, clockwise.

Surely enough, to my utter disbelief, those squiggly symbols started to appear, all the way back around to where the number sequence started… at 1. I withdrew my hand in disgust.

"To hell with this, mate," I said to Mark, "this is all wrong. That dial was - is - a circle. It went from 1 through to 9 and back to 1. I saw it."

"Yeah, mad that there's all that stuff there now… looks like an alien language or something," he said, in wonder.

"No, listen," I went on, panicking a bit, "you're missing the point. It's a circle. It's the same size. The dimensions won't have changed, but it's got… more symbols on it. Mark, there's more fucking circle than there was last time we were here."

I watched Mark's brow furrow, and then his jaw hung agape as the penny dropped.

"That's impossible," he said.

"Aye. It should be. I mean, maybe it's…" I floundered for an explanation that wouldn't break the laws of geometry, "a different dial? A one with a wider circumference that we just think is the same size as the old one?"

"Who would have been in here to change it, though?"

I was troubled. I was scared. "Nobody," I admitted to myself, "it's clearly the same dial. It's fixed into the wall, innit."

We walked out of the room. Mark picked up the notebook, began to leaf through it, muttering to himself.

"What are we going to do about this? I feel like this is enough to tell Professor Prestwick… if we've managed to break the known laws of geometry and physics already. Surely?"

Mark continued to mutter to himself.

"Mark?"

No reply, just the constant page-turning and muttering. His eyes were wide and wild.

"Oh, for God's sake, not you as well," I said, exasperated.

Mark, wordlessly, showed me a combination of numbers and symbols that Scott had drawn circles around and underlined several times, in the back of the book.

"Yes?" I asked, "what does it mean?"

"I don't know," said Mark, "let's find out. Let's enter these numbers and symbols, I'm sure we can find them on the dial."

"No, God, don't, this is too weird. The dial shouldn't be big enough to hold those symbols, but it bloody well does. Can't you see how wrong this is? Let's put it all down and go find the Professor. Maybe one of the faculty members knows how to get hold of him, maybe they've got his mobile number. Mark? Mark!"

I watched as he got up, zombie-like, eyes fixed on the notebook in his hands, and walked into the vanta-room. I pleaded with him to stop but he merely pointed at the sequence on the page, tapping it with his pen. Glumly, I listened for the clicks I knew were coming as he entered the sequence: click, click, click, click, click... click.

After these six clicks of the dial, Mark came out of the black room and hovered his finger over the button outside it.

"Curiosity killed the cat," I said half-heartedly. I should have stopped him, I know, but... I wanted to know for myself too. I was merely putting up a show of being hesitant, too cowardly to press the button myself and too curious to stop Mark from doing it.

After a moment's delay and a deep breath, Mark pushed the button.

What happened next was the most bizarre thing yet - the oscillating noise ripped open my ears, but I also felt it in every inch of my body. My teeth felt as though they'd rattle out of my skull. I even held my hands to my face instinctively, such was my conviction that they'd fall right out of my mouth. My vision was blurred and didn't come back to normal for some time. There were patches of black swimming over my field of view. Things were coming in and out of focus, and bizarre visual distortions of solid objects made them wiggle and wave as though they were underwater.

I had to shout to hear myself over the ensuing tinnitus: "What was THAT?"

"PROGRESS!" Mark shouted in return, with that gleeful spark in his eye. I looked over to where he stood with the notebook, frantically writing down everything that the screen displayed.

I didn't know what to say except, "I'm off to look for Prestwick."

Mark ignored me, and I nearly ripped the door out of its frame in my desperation to get out of the room. It had begun to fill with that smell, that strange, unplaceable chemical eggy smell, and I had to get some air.

But I was out of luck. The smell followed me everywhere. I bumbled through the corridor that led out of our little room, while black patches appeared all over the walls and slid onto the floor, and I crashed through the other doors into the basement laboratory. I was having trouble walking in a straight line, my balance was so badly affected by the ringing noise in my ears. It was like being very drunk, but with none of the accompanying good-humouredness.

I moved through the basement laboratory and up the stairs with a panicked urgency, sensing that something was very wrong. This wasn't simply wrong in the way that Professor Prestwick smiled in a strange way, this was… something else.

Distances felt weird, the stairs took longer to get to than they should have done, and the walls were too far away. The stairs themselves seemed to have gained an extra flight, and more than once, it felt as though I were going downward rather than upward. I put this down to being in a rush, I must have gone through a different door or something, I wasn't thinking straight.

I barged through another set of double-doors, and I tried to make sense of what I saw in front of me. This was not the same old Physics department that I'd walked through. The corridor ahead stretched off way too far into the distance, with way too many doors all down one side. I couldn't see the end; it disappeared into infinity. But it was still, ostensibly, the same department: same floor-tiles, same walls, same doors… but the length and the amount of doors were wrong.

The more I looked, the more disturbing things that I saw. Long windows ran down the opposite side of the corridor. We were up on the third floor, but there were doors between some of these windows. Doors… to nowhere. We were so many floors up, and there were doors to the outside… I shook my head. As I peered down the corridor, I noted that some of the doors were wonky, diagonal, with their bottom corners disappearing into the floor.

And of course, outside the windows, a vanta-black sky glowered, all-encompassing and oppressive. It was morning mere hours ago. Was it now night time? Or was it something else entirely? I was drenched in a cold sweat now. This was nightmarish. I didn't want to go down this corridor, but I didn't want to go back to mad Mark in the lab, either.

Underneath my feet, I felt a rumbling. Dull at first, slow, but then, a faster thumping... almost as though a very deep sound wave was oscillating.

"Oh, shit," I said aloud, and walked over to the nearest wall. I braced myself against it. Mark had obviously been busy down in the basement; he'd set off another abyssal sound wave, one which reached its peak as I stood there and left me gasping for breath.

There were deafening sounds, not just from the oscillating wave, but of moving masonry, rock rumbling around me and beneath me, and the squeal of glass contorting but not quite smashing. The corridor I stood in shook, and I fell to the floor despite my strong position against the wall. When I stood up, I looked around in confusion.

The corridor was back to normal. The sky outside was still black - too black for mere night-time, though. I began to suspect that wherever I was, whatever this was, perhaps the regular rules of day and night were not being followed as rigidly as I was used to. The laws of geometry certainly weren't.

I thought, oddly, that the corridor's dishevelled appearance before the latest sound-wave from the machine was almost like a sketch, with its odd doors to nowhere and diagonal frames. After the noise, it appeared to have shaped up quite nicely.

Not wanting to go backwards, and seeing little reason to go outside under that horrible vanta-black sky, I walked down the corridor. At least, I thought, I might be able to find someone that could help. I wanted to find Professor Prestwick, but whether I'd ask him for help when I found him, or just throttle him for pulling me into this damned project, I didn't know.

I pushed my way through the door that usually led to the undergraduate laboratory, not fully expecting that it would still lead there. Thankfully, it did, and I found myself in the lab that I usually walked through on my way to Prestwick's office.

It looked about right, in terms of decor and dimensions, but I noticed that a couple of the workbenches and the stools were on the ceiling. They didn't appear to be falling to the earth, as they should have done.

"That's gravity broken as well as time as time and space, then," I said aloud.

"Broken, indeed," came a sad, wobbly voice from behind me.

I turned around with a start.

In front of me was a horrible, amorphous blob, hunched over one of the workbenches that was still bolted to the floor. There were scattered notebooks everywhere, absolutely covered in the alien symbols that had appeared on the dial in the vanta-room below, and too many hands holding too many biro pens, each with too many fingers.

Looking out at me, in a saggy, deflated fashion, was the pale face of Scott. Obviously, he had not gone home. I looked at him in abject horror, my mouth hanging agape. His face looked as though it had been printed upon a balloon, inflated to thrice its normal size, and then allowed to slowly deflate into a rumpled-up mess.

There were too many limbs, too many body parts in general. I hated what I saw in front of me, I was revolted, I was frightened - and worst of all I felt a pang of tragic sadness in my stomach. This thing used to be Scott.

The thing opened its mouth and said, in a very off-pitch approximation of Scott's voice, "you left me for a very long time."

"What?" I said, moving away from it, "how long? We were gone for one night!"

"I don't know, weeks, months, years... I don't think time works the same here."

"I don't think time is working properly, either, but what do you mean here? Where are we?"

"We're... there, where Prestwick wanted us to be."

"What is all this, what happened to you!?" I yelled, panicking.

"Prestwick's machine... the frequencies... we haven't been measuring frequencies. We've been tuning them."

"Tuning... to what?" I remembered, then - that Prestwick had mentioned this last time I saw him, in passing. He slipped that one under the radar, and I wish I'd paid more attention to his wording at the time.

Scott answered, "Well, I'm not quite sure I could describe it in words you'd understand... the things I've seen, though..." Scott said dreamily, mentally wandering off.

Secretly, I had been walking backward toward a lab stool. I fully planned to use this as a weapon if Scott got any closer, and he did appear to be slipping and sliding over the floor towards me, albeit very slowly and awkwardly.

"What have we been tuning to, Scott?"

"Do you not see? We've been tuning to a different place... we've been tuning in to a different place entirely. A different world, a different plane, a different reality..."

"What the hell are you on about?"

"Or we may be tuning into a different physical part of our own universe... but I hope not... I hope nothing like this exists in our universe..." he said, with a tinge of sadness. The wobbly, oscillating frequency of his voice gave it a most unsettling sing-song quality.

"Scott, shut up and talk sense, maybe I can help you. Tell me what's going on!"

"I can't be helped, none of us can... the research has progressed too far. We've completed too much of the tuning process, can't you see? We're resonating. Prestwick isn't Prestwick, he's being used... one of them is wearing his skin."

"You're really scaring me now, Scott," I said, stalling for time, "who do you mean, them?"

At this point, I was fully willing to believe him, but I didn't trust him for a moment. He meant me harm, I was sure of it. I needed to get a grip on that stool and put more distance between us. I wasn't sure where the light source was in this room, but the shadows of his too-many limbs were reaching high, all over the walls, all over the ceiling. It felt like a spider was encroaching upon me, and I was trapped in its web.

"I'm not sure who or what they are... sentient beings, certainly.

They seek out worlds like ours… they scan for certain frequencies, certain signals that are indicative of advanced civilisations. Civilisations capable of splitting the atom, of particle acceleration… civilisations like ours. Humanity."

"Why?"

"Well, the answer is simple enough. We are their prey. They find a way in, they warp reality around certain individuals, but they can't all come through at once… it's like planting a seed. At first, their influence is too small, they can only do so much… they can prick reality, maybe cause a strange result in an experiment, cause gravity to work a bit differently, and lead people down stranger and stranger paths." Scott's sad head tilted to the side as he continued, and a couple of his arms gestured around the lab, "here, they found people like Prestwick, people who were too curious for their own good, fed them rogue lines of computer code, rogue results, and led them down strange avenues of research until they saw an opportunity to possess them entirely."

"Oh," I said, pacing backward, "well that would explain some of Prestwick's behaviour. But how do you know all this?"

"I've seen it all, I've a window into their psyche now… I fear I'm being taken over myself. My mind is no longer just my own, I have memories I cannot possibly understand, memories of dimensions my human brain can't digest… but half of me does understand it, my friend. Half of me does understand."

He lurched towards me now, and I dodged backward, grabbing the stool and holding it in front of me. The shadows on the walls reached towards me and tugged at me, grabbed at my arms, pulled backward on my legs, took me off guard and tipped me onto my back. I cracked my head on the hard floor and saw stars for a moment.

I threw them off, as their grip wasn't very strong. They were like jelly. I scrambled backwards and looked back at the shadows - they weren't shadows at all! More like flat limbs that all emanated from the central Scott-monstrosity at their centre. I screamed with the sheer horror of realising that these very limbs had been crawling all over the walls and ceiling.

There were too many of them - way too many - and I decided to bolt for the nearest door. It should take me further down the same corridor I was in, I thought, but who knows where I'd actually end up.

Scott rambled on, his sad, sunken face apparently completely unaware of what his alien body was doing.

"After they possessed a few key figures, they set those figures to work, tuning our frequencies so that they may bring their world closer to ours... look around you, look at the sky. We're halfway there already. Wherever they're from, it's cold, it's dark, it's dead... no light..."

There was no need to reply. I ran for the door.

Scott went on, "we're tuning our world to theirs. We're meshing our realities, resonating together. For every signal sent from Earth, there is a reply... you must understand, they are actively tuning their world to ours, too. You may have noticed that they don't quite get it right the first time, things might be upside-down, or the laws of physics don't work properly..."

Or they can't smile properly, or operate a human body properly, I thought hastily. Scott's bizarre version of events would certainly explain things better than anything I could have thought of, impossible though it seemed. I threw open the door to the lab, went through, and slammed it behind me, sick of Scott's disturbing chatter and sickened by the thought of sharing his fate.

I fell three feet downward.

I had ended up in the same corridor as before - however, it was, as Scott had warned, upside-down now. I stood on the ceiling - the dangling light bulbs that lit the place were now suspended in the air at knee-height, as though they were levitating. Gravity still appeared to be pointing towards the floor-tiles; however, it didn't have an effect on me.

My body mustn't have been part of the strange tuning experiment being performed by some incomprehensible being in another reality... only the corridor. Was that really the case? Was there something in another... plane? Another reality? Another universe? Or something incomprehensibly far away, doing the same kind of experiments that we had been doing, in direct correspondence with ours?

I shook my head to remove these bizarre notions from my head and ran to the end of the corridor that I'd come through. I managed to open the door, upside-down, with some level of awkwardness and pile through into the staircase that led to the basement.

Gravity was working correctly here, and I fell to the ground rather unceremoniously, landing on my hands and knees. My stomach lurched as my insides caught up with the inversion, as though I'd just been tipped upside-down on a roller-coaster.

I ran through the basement lab, which was warping before my very eyes, where the eggy chemical reek made my eyes water. I'd reached the tunnel before the basement sub-room where I'd left Mark. My first thoughts were of escaping with him, so I'd immediately made a beeline for him, without realising what a daft idea this might have been. Truth be told, I don't know where we would have escaped to - we could have run forever under the vanta-black sky, with no hope of seeing our own sun rise again, ever fearful of dropping into the void.

I nearly booted the door off its hinges on my way into the vanta-room.

"MARK!" I shouted, "MARK! We're leaving!"

In here, the eggy stench was truly nauseating, and there was no doubt in my mind that it emanated from whatever this horrible machine was doing. I cast my eyes around for Mark but couldn't see him. There were multiple notepads sprawled all over the desk, all over the floor, spent pens strewn all over everything.

I'd been away longer than I thought, obviously. Time did not work here. My stomach sank as I thought about what had happened to Scott after too much "research" and "tuning" with that damned machine... could the same have happened to Mark?

My mind raced. It was here that I started piecing together the puzzle: the extent of how long we'd been away, the gigantic pile of letters in the doorway, the ginger lad talking to us as if we'd been away for ages, the vanta-black skies on our walk home.

I realised, with a level of terror that eclipsed even what I felt when I saw the Scott-strosity in the undergraduate labs, that Mark and I had been tuned to elsewhere when we had walked home that evening, after Scott had caused the first oscillation event by pushing the button. I realised that, after I heard that oscillating noise, I had been "out of tune", and the streets I walked, my own house even, were just a frail copy, a poor imagining of our own world, which explained why there was nobody around and it all felt so lifeless. If I'd gone and knocked at any of the doors, entered any of the houses, who knows what I'd have seen... there'd have been nobody home, I know that much.

Would I have seen poor approximations of their interiors, diagonal doorframes, furniture on the ceiling, infinite corridors? Or just a terrifying, vanta-black void?

The reverse-noise that I heard in my sleep, the one that started out high and ended low in pitch, that was me tuning back into the proper reality that I was used to... but sleeping in that bizarre netherworld must have been weeks-long "outside", in the "real world". With the things I'd seen in the last hour, my definition of "real world" had shifted significantly, but it's still the best way I can describe it.

It was with some consternation that I thought about what Mark had done by entering that sequence and pressing the button - apparently more than once - effectively re-tuning us to that netherworld, to an even closer degree than before. Prestwick's words flashed in my memory then: "...do it again. Rotate the dial again, differently, more. Keep doing it."

"What a bastard," I muttered aloud. I still couldn't find my overly-curious friend anywhere. Mark might have taken his leave, I hoped. Or maybe he was like Scott now, poring over notebooks in the labs... but surely I'd have seen him, I'd have passed him on the way.

Or would I, I thought to myself, when the laws of time and

geometry are so thoroughly warped? He could be anywhere, he could be anywhen.

I walked over to the desk and looked at the notebooks... there were a ton of sequences scrawled upon the pages, with at least ten, maybe twenty circled frantically. Had he managed to cause this many oscillation events while I was away? I'd only experienced one, but nothing seemed to follow any kind of logic here, so I guessed that the circled ones must have been "good results".

I shook my head. Our regular, human numbers had all but disappeared, with the majority of these sequences being made up entirely of those wriggly figures that seemed so offensive to the human psyche. Mark had clearly surpassed Scott in his contributions to Prestwick's project, then, I thought with bitter irony.

I cast another look around, to see if he was lurking in the shadows, or if he was lying somewhere injured. I saw nothing.

And then I heard it: click.

A most curious, and yet terribly familiar noise... I looked around in panic, wondering what had made the noise, trying to work out what sounded so recognisable.

Click.

There it was again. My head turned slowly, in trepidation, towards the vanta-room. The door was ajar.

Click.

I could feel my pulse in my throat, and my stomach was churning. My jaw hung slack and I shook my head: no, no, no.

The dial - the fucking dial!

Mark was in there, turning the dial!

Click.

"MARK! STOP!" I screamed, and ran towards the door of the vanta-room. I got there just as I heard the fifth turn of the dial: click. There was only one left before the sequence would be completed.

I burst through the door and rounded the corner into the inky darkness of the room enclosed within its vanta-black walls and looked around feverishly, trying to see Mark, but he wasn't in front of the dial where I expected him to be.

"MARK! What's going on, where is he," I said to myself, "am I going mad or what?"

"Oh, we're all mad here," came a voice from above, "Prestwick's led us down the rabbit hole, I'm afraid."

I looked up; the vanta-black ceiling made it hard to discern anything… but I did see the remains of a lab coat, torn into tatters, hanging down from the ceiling against the black. It was hard to see anything in here, but dim light from the doorway illuminated the strips of white fabric just enough.

What were they hanging from, though? I couldn't see. I looked around, and my eyes landed on the disfigured remnants of Mark's face. The face was much too far away from the lab coat for my liking; it was in one of the top corners of the room, dimly lit from the same light in the doorway, so that I could only see a pale oval and some darker holes where the eyes and mouth would be.

The mouth-hole was too big.

It moved, "You left me for quite a while, there… but don't worry. I understand. Time's not quite what it seems any more, is it?"

I gulped and made my way back towards the door in the most surreptitious way that I could manage.

"I made a lot of progress, you know. And I was rewarded handsomely. I care not for the money, the fame any more… I have received knowledge that far surpasses any of that. The small portion of my consciousness that belonged to 'Mark' is now but a fraction of my memories… I have beheld vistas the likes of which would drive you mad, my friend."

His head jerked, he began to move, he dripped from the ceiling from limbs which I could only assume were so black that they blended in with the walls, and could have stretched everywhere, much like Scott's.

I remembered what happened with Scott reaching behind me, and dropped all pretence of stealth. I turned around and ran, pushing away horribly gelatinous limbs which made attempts to grab me and subdue me, all the way to the door.

As I crossed the threshold, I heard it, the horrible and final sixth turn of the dial.

Click.

A change came over the atmosphere in the room, a horrible potential seemed to have charged the air... whatever "it" was, it was ready to go. I wanted to close the door behind me, but I felt as though I was pushed out by a hundred hands. On reflection, there could well have been that many. I fell to the floor on my face and scrambled forward, rolling over to end up on my feet.

A horrendous mockery of Mark emerged from the doorway, all spidery limbs and gelatinous goo, and shadows that reached to the ceiling and around the walls darted toward me with alarming speed. I ran toward the door to the basement, but, in a flash, shadowy limbs pulled the main body of Mark towards the doorway so that he ended up in front of it, blocking my path.

I was forced to look into his eyes; you will not be surprised to hear that they were an unnerving shade of blacker-than-black. His face, like Scott's, was oddly deflated and out of shape, but it was definitely him. He was in even worse shape than Scott, though, and he seemed malevolent, in contrast to Scott's sadness. He looked at me like I was - well, like I was prey.

He licked his lips - with two tongues, the likes of which I can scarcely describe - and darted towards me. I dived to the right, towards the computer desks, and threw an office chair in his direction. It had little effect: rather than the satisfying thud I had expected, it was more of a splash, as though I'd thrown it into a wall of water.

I heard a guttural chuckle, and looked behind me to see his horrific visage smiling an un-smile, reminiscent of the Professor's. I looked around in blind panic; there was nothing I could do against a foe such as this. I resorted to pleading.

"Mark," I said, "are you not still in there? Stop! Let me help you! Let's put a stop to this!"

"Oh, I'm still in here," he said, slithering towards me on a black mass which took up most of the floor, "but I told you already,

'Mark' occupies such a small place amongst the infinite space I have now had the privilege to comprehend… I would share my experiences, if only you'd let me!"

"Get away," I shouted, "you look like you want to devour me!"

"Well," said Mark, smiling the un-smile once more, "how do you think I learned about it all?"

At this, I gave up on the idea of negotiating and tried to sabotage the machine in a last ditch attempt to ruin Prestwick's project and, well, save the world. I began wildly pulling at the terminals, pulling panels off computers, throwing monitors in the direction of Mark, who moved towards me all the while.

"Stop," he said, "you waste your energy. The work is already done. They are attuned - it isn't just here, you know. It's not just Aldwich University, either - it's everywhere. Almost every other major University has been doing exactly what we've been doing, at Prestwick's behest."

"SHUT UP!" I screamed, not wanting to accept it.

"We've installed them everywhere, even CERN. Almost all of the world's research facilities are dedicating their computational power to Prestwick's project, and it has all but reached its completion… they are here. We are there. Our frequencies are all but matched - near-perfect resonation."

"Why?" I asked, sweating, looking for any route of escape.

"It's what we desire," he said, his voice now modulated to an impossibly low frequency, "energy. It's what we seek. Civilisations that put out these levels of power, these frequencies, these markers that betray them so… we are no different to sharks that hunt fish in your oceans. You have shown yourselves to your predators, and your time runs out as the walls get thinner."

After a second's delay, Mark, or the otherworldly entity that possessed him, lunged for me. I ducked out of the way, pushed forwards, and fought my way through wet rubbery limbs, barely able to see, until I got free of them and grabbed the nearest solid object I could: a door.

I pushed through it and slammed it behind me, hoping to see

the concrete corridor that led to the basement, but what I saw instead was utter blackness. Vanta-blackness.

"NO!" I shouted, as I realised what I'd done - in my haste and blindness, I had blundered into the vanta-room. I was within the very hub of this awful tuning experiment, which was primed to go, loaded with a combination of six alien characters…

And Mark was outside. I stood up, reached towards the handle, but my hand seemed to move impossibly slowly…

I heard a percussive noise from outside the room that seemed to shake the very foundations of the floor. Mark had pushed the button.

What happened next was impossible to describe. I felt like I had been transported through aeons, through entire vistas of space, with my entire being, my entire soul, reverberating as though oscillating in response to the noises that the machine produced.

I saw things I cannot remember without wailing, things so utterly disturbing that they reduced all earthly concerns to nothing… I witnessed inconceivable civilisations reduced to rubble and devoured, I saw stars wink out one-by-one, so that skies were left dark and cold, vanta-black.

I saw masses of teeming black limbs stretching out across the cosmos, feeling, sensing, watching for certain frequencies… hungering.

Eventually, the noise reached its high-pitched peak, and I was left on the floor of the room, exhausted. How long had it been? I had no idea. Timidly, I pushed open the door. Something told me Mark had gotten exactly what he wanted, and that I no longer needed to fear him.

I did not feel quite myself.

I looked around the room - still the same scene of chaos, but no Mark. Gingerly, I walked toward the door, my head buzzing, the chemical stench high in my nostrils, the walls warping in and out as though made of jelly, and made my way out to the Physics department to confront whatever awaited me there.

What happened next is but a daze, a hazy dream to me now. I had one main thing on my mind: find Prestwick. Failing that: escape.

I pressed on, navigating corridors that had adopted almost realistic approximations of their real dimensions. There were still some oddities, black patches here and there, doorways to no-where, the odd light fixture hanging upside-down on the floor, but the layout was largely intact.

This sounds relieving, but no, not at all. I thought, with a shud-der, that the tuning was very much nearing completion. I looked out of a window to see a vanta-black sky. Was I on Earth? Had my world been transported there, to a cold, dead, devoured sky? In that case, why was gravity working, why had I not frozen to death from a sky that lacked sunlight? Had their world come here? Was I somewhere in-between?

I stood and looked out of the window, hypnotised, having lost all hope of returning to normality. I was awoken from my reverie by a tap on the shoulder, and turned around to see Mark.

Just plain old Mark - a human with the usual amount of limbs and fingers, and a face that looked almost normal, apart from the eyes.

"Hello, old friend."

"Hi," I said glumly. I should have killed him where he stood, but I was rather deflated at that point. I felt like I'd lost already.

"Good to see you on board with the project."

"What?" I said, confused.

"You're much more… agreeable than you were when we last met. Sorry about setting the machine off while you were in there, old chum, but you know - the work must go on. I wasn't sure you'd made it."

"How long was I in there?"

"Well," said Mark, smiling an un-smile, "can't really say. A long time."

"You tried to eat me, I think," I accused.

"You were prey, then, friend. Not so much now."

"Ah," I said, not willing to continue the conversation any further. I felt as though my bones had been squashed underneath a cement-roller. I turned around and made to hobble away from him, unwilling to even look at him. Somehow, it was still disturbing to see him in human form - I knew it wasn't him. Whatever had taken hold of him, whatever was using him as a vessel, had completed its tuning operation and had a much better hold over him now.

There were no shadowy tangled limbs - but I knew that that's what he was. It wore him well, I thought, sickened.

I walked away, with him blathering in the background - I tried not to hear any of it. As I rounded a corner, I heard him shout, "Where are you going?"

"To find Prestwick," I shouted back, and coughed a little. My body had really been put through the wringer in the vanta-room.

"Hah! I don't think he's receiving visitors," came the answer.

I pushed on regardless. I reached the undergraduate laboratories, aiming to take the shortcut through them to Prestwick's office.

I saw Scott in there, looking better than ever, with blacker-than-black eyes, with a clipboard. He was taking measurements with various instruments, smiling and nodding, and writing down the results. He looked at me and smiled - as I'm sure you can guess, a deeply unwholesome smile.

"Ah, great to see you, my friend," he said, waving. "Come and join in the research. Prestwick's project nears its completion."

"Piss off," I said, pushing past him.

Scott laughed, "Join in, my friend, don't fight it. Can you not see?"

"Can I not see what?"

Scott looked at me, black eyes twinkling. "You're part of the project now whether you like it or not. You're resonating. It'll follow you wherever you go... better you stay here. The rewards are considerable."

I considered his words for a minute, before repeating myself, "Piss off."

I pushed through the labs and moved towards the corridor that contained Prestwick's office. On my way, I passed a fire exit and decided to push through it out of curiosity. I ended up on a first floor outdoor walkway, a fire-escape, which led down to one of the car parks. All fairly normal - I'd have expected that - except for the cold, dead, vanta-black sky above me. I looked at it and shook my head. It was all I could do; it was no use screaming at the sky, was it?

I walked out some distance onto the walkway, which stretched on forever, before deciding this was a fruitless effort. I turned around and looked back at the building.

My jaw dropped.

Set against the black sky, the normally angular Brutalist bridges and jutting balconies of the Physics department were completely haywire. There were too many bridges, jutting out at awkward angles, they looked to be moving as though they were the limbs of some twisted creature. The whole building was contorting, entire corridors came free of their surrounds and joined other corridors at impossible angles, angles which would give a protractor nightmares. All over the outside of the building were shadowy lines, with no light-source… they were probably the limbs of those things, I realised.

I was horrified, but oddly fascinated. I hate to say it, but I did feel privileged to be able to see such a majestic display of alien, geometry-bending horror, while the culprits apparently no longer saw me as a threat, or even as food. I beheld things that no other human has ever beheld. I watched for longer than I care to admit.

I watched through the windows as other faculty members walked around with clipboards, tapping walls, measuring things, writing down their results. I watched their counterparts on the outside crawl and slither across the outer walls, presumably doing the same.

Obviously, the outdoors still had some tuning to do, whereas the indoors were done already. This made me feel a small sense of relief, actually - if the outdoors were still in this state, and it was only the Physics departments and various Universities and research facilities across the world that had been fully assimilated... then there was still time.

Time to do what, though? I snorted at the futility of it all. I feared Scott was right - why fight it? I listened, and surely enough, I could hear pronging noises of different volumes, pinging oscillations from every direction in the sky. Everywhere with one of Prestwick's machines, I surmised, all tuning themselves in to impossible frequencies, impossible dimensions.

There was a door to my left, I realised, along the outdoor walkway. I peeked around its frame, until I could see the other side of it - another door to nowhere. Out of pure curiosity, I opened it. Inside, I saw a mass of teeming limbs stretched across shifting geometry, a thousand alien faces, deflated and sad, all looking toward the newly opened door.

At once, they set off, moving toward me. I laughed a maniacal laugh and slammed the door in their faces. Now truly maddened, I wandered back into the building, my head buzzing with a mixture of adrenaline and amusement.

I walked towards Prestwick's office. Maybe I'd get some pleasure out of stabbing the bastard, I thought. Or, maybe, I realised with some excitement, if I could kill him, it would put an end to all of this. Maybe the whole project would run to ground if it was leaderless.

I broke into a jog, moving until I saw the shiny plaque on the door, emblazoned: PROF. PRESTWICK.

I took a deep breath and turned the handle.

I saw Prestwick there, hunched over a terminal in the far corner. This was no ordinary terminal, though. It was like an unholy pulpit, made of writhing blocks emblazoned with symbols that I recognised from the machine's dial and the notebooks. His two human hands rested on either side, but the blocks were being manipulated by something invisible... I knew what: shadowy limbs that he had grown adept at hiding.

He turned around, somewhat surprised at the intrusion.

"I requested no disturbances," he said, until he recognised me.

I stared at him, boggle-eyed and exhausted.

"Ah! The man of the hour," he said, "do you care to join your colleagues in finishing my project? Do you desire knowledge beyond your wildest dreams?"

"No," I said and looked around the room for some kind of weapon.

"No? Well whatever are you here for, then?" He wasn't being arch - he sounded genuinely taken aback. As though it would indeed be my privilege to continue working for him, to become assimilated into an awful entity from beyond the veil. My eyes rested on a heavy book - the best I could do. I picked it up and walked towards him, murder in my eyes.

"Ah, come now, surely you can't be so dense," he said.

I lifted up the book and made to bludgeon him with it.

Invisible limbs took the book from my hands, wrapped themselves around me, and threw me against the far wall.

Prestwick walked towards me. He smiled his un-smile. "You know everything, but you do not realise. You've gathered the data, but you have not yet internalised the results. Do you not see? We have won. There wasn't even a battle. We are everywhere, we are too many, we have penetrated too deeply. It may take some time, but eventually your world will be devoured, and from there, even your stars will wink out of the sky. It's over."

I merely sighed in response. Unlike his counterparts, his limbs were strong and held me fast. I thought, at that moment, that I would die.

"You've seen us for what we are, anyway, no need to keep up the charade."

With this, he flickered for a moment, and I screamed. The creature before me no longer possessed Professor Prestwick's form nor wore the face of any other being. For the first time, I truly beheld the naked face of one of these entities, and I screamed until my throat was raw.

There were many things which I suppose could be called mouths - and all of them smiled. There were no teeth, nor facial muscles to join in with the smiles, but I definitely think of them all as smiling Prestwick's un-smile regardless.

My eyes darted toward the coat-stand that I had seen previously, the first time I entered his office. I'd sworn I'd seen something there. Now, hanging on a hook, as though discarded like a wet jacket, was the empty, clammy skin of Professor Prestwick, with desperately hollow eyes looking at me, imploring me to help him.

I couldn't. I screamed with tears in my eyes, held stiff against the wall.

The face came close, surveyed me from left and right, up and down.

"Yes," came a disembodied voice, which sounded nothing like Prestwick's. The voice sounded foreign, alien, but still used Prestwick's English as though it were a habit that had proved hard to shake.

It spoke once more: "We may have use for you yet..."

With this, one of the thing's shadowy limbs procured a strange six-pronged device from the pulpit behind it. It had a handle at the bottom, which was gripped by one of the entity's thin black tentacle-like protrusions. It looked, for all the world, like a six-pronged tuning fork.

The limbs brought it high, and struck it back down against the pulpit. There was an incredibly loud high-pitched tone as the six prongs of alien metal resonated with each other, and I realised the sound was moving oddly back and forth, oscillating, getting lower in pitch...

It continued oscillating, until the movement was felt rather than heard, and with a massive booming rumble, much like I had experienced while asleep, I was detuned from that nightmare netherworld, and the sensation of it knocked me out cold.

I awoke in the corridor outside Prestwick's office, on a bench. I felt awful, but much to my relief, it was daylight outside the window. I rushed up to look - the streets outside looked normal, there were cars, people, pigeons, clouds, the sun.

I laughed, daring for a moment to believe that everything had been some sort of fiendish fever dream - until I turned around.

Standing in a line were Professor Prestwick, Mark, Scott, the ginger lad, and the other two students who had left with him. There were a few other faculty members too.

Mark and the lads were all smiling their horrendous un-smiles, which unsettled me deeply. I knew they were no longer themselves. But what unnerved me most of all was Professor Prestwick; he was smiling rather normally. I realised, with horror, that the very advanced entity which had possessed Prestwick had finally learned how to make him smile.

How could I trust anybody again, knowing that they were capable of such total mimicry? He looked completely human. I gasped and stood still, unable to even run. My hopes were dashed.

Prestwick moved toward me and held out a piece of paper - which I took. I looked down at it: a cheque.

"Your payment, as promised," Prestwick said, with a hatefully warm smile.

On the wall, I noticed that a fire extinguisher was in fact upside-down. Could have been placed there in error, or...

"Fuck off," I said, "no way..."

"That's hardly a way to thank me, but it's an understandable response. Why don't you fuck off, as you so eloquently put it, and spend your money while the time still allows? Your colleagues here," he gestured towards the un-smiling freaks, "have decided that they will join me. They will live forever, assimilated into consciousnesses so vast as to experience limitless sensation, to explore every corner of numerous realities, to satisfy immense hungers that you could scarcely imagine."

I was silent. I had no response.

He grinned a toothier, more carnivorous smile now, "And you, you chose otherwise. You will run for the rest of your life, which will not be long, and you will attempt to tell folk who will dismiss

you out of hand, who will call you insane. Did you choose correctly, my friend? Time will tell."

At this, he bade his freaks to stand aside, and I walked away
stiffly, my mind numbed by what I had so recently experienced.

I heard him say one last thing: "Enjoy the money, my friend. It
is a rather handsome amount, as promised. You could go anywhere - anywhere on Earth, that is."

I walked out of the University, which seemed to be full of beam-
ing freaks, all smiling un-smiles at me, all carrying clipboards, all
in on it... or were they just students, carrying their files to their
next lecture? I could not be convinced of my hold on my sanity,
and this was the wrong place for me to be, so I went home.

The cheque was indeed handsome, and I immediately used it
to escape as far away as possible. I flew everywhere, anywhere...
unable to escape the memories or the dreams of thin limbs and
vanta-black skies.

Anywhere I went, I made sure it was far away from research facilities and busy University towns. Hotels, lodges, guest-houses...
all of them would serve me well at first, and I did what I could to
enjoy myself and forget what I had seen. I almost told somebody
my story in a hotel bar, once... but I decided against it. Even blind
drunk, I had not the courage to spin somebody such a yarn.

These places were all nice at first, normal... but I'd wake up in
the night. Was it just dark, or were there patches of black ap-
pearing on the walls? I could never tell. A few times, I thought I
saw the night-sky looking too black, little patches of vanta-black
against starry skies like an awful patchwork quilt.

I decided to move more quickly, never staying anywhere for
long. I'd sleep somewhere and wake up days later - and staff
members would be missing. One time, I woke up in the night,
and wanted to go down to the bar... but there was nobody there.
Nobody in the whole building, in fact. The more I looked closely
at paintings on the wall, the more I could see that they were... off.
Or upside-down.

Shaking my head - no, no, no, - I ran back to my bedroom and buried my head under the blankets, and tried my best to sleep it off.

All was well in the morning - but the staff behaved rather strangely. I began to observe stranger and stranger headlines coming out of newspapers from the cities, and yet the strange events seemed to happen closer and closer to the rural idylls that I'd fled to.

Scott's words flashed up in my memory then: "You're part of the project now whether you like it or not. You're resonating. It'll follow you wherever you go…"

And Prestwick's: "we may have use for you yet…"

I had not escaped at all. I've realised the answer to a question which has been bugging me ever since I left the University: why did they just let me leave? I had convinced myself it was just a sadistic thing, that they got some perverse pleasure from the fact that nobody would believe me, or that they were honour-bound to uphold their end of the deal and pay me for fair work.

I should have known better.

I've been carrying it with me. I'm fully tuned. I'm resonating. Anywhere I go, it happens, and that's why I was allowed to leave. I've been doing their work for them, the bastards. I've been spreading it! Wherever I go, I help them cover more ground, help them establish new links, help them tune into more of our poor planet.

We don't stand a chance. I don't know what I'm going to do, in the end, but I fear the end will come soon. I write this document as a kind of confession. But to what end? Who will even read it before the end comes? And who would believe it? The paper this is written on - much like everything else - will be devoured, swallowed, by fiendish entities from realms far outside our understanding.

Humanity, all of our grand achievements, our art, our history… we were but prey. And our supposed scientific "progress" led us directly to our predators. Our civilisation and our stars will wink out, and the black void will expand outwards forever, as light and life fall under the writhing tide.

Credits

Dave Martel
Editor-in-Chief
- host of "THE BOG" on YouTube, channel: DaveMartel
- project manager for The Epicist magazine (Norroena.org)
- Creator of Grimeorth Roleplaying game (Amazon)
- Telegram & Twitter t.me/TheBoglord

Cyprus Walter
Lead Editor and Book Layout
- The Midgard Institute: themidgardinstitute.wordpress.com
- Midgard Poetry: midgardpoetry.wordpress.com

A. Cuthbertson
Featured Author

Light of Decay
Cover Art & Layout

Michael Sagginario
Book Layout
- Irminfolk Odinist Community: Irminfolk.com

for more publications, info about the pulp genre, and much more, visit our website:

thebizarchives.com

for live updates & announcements, follow us on Telegram & Twitter:

@theBizArchives

Manufactured by Amazon.ca
Bolton, ON

27921479R00055